OUTLASTING AFTER

BOOK 1 OUTLASTING SERIES

LK MAGILL

FIRST HALE PRESS

Outlasting After/ LK Magill – 1st ed.

Ebook ISBN 978-1-7336155-4-9

Paperback ISBN 978-1-7336155-5-6

Hardcover ISBN 978-1-950928-05-7

DEDICATION_

To God, thank you for allowing me to write another.

ACKNOWLEDGMENTS_

I don't mean to beat the same drum... but the same people just keep helping me. I guess I'm very fortunate that way. So in no particular order, a huge thank you goes out to:

My mother/therapist/cheer leader, Jan. Your fierce support is awesome, awesome, awesome.

My early readers... Ali, Sara, Jenna and Chae. Your enthusiasm, insight and honesty has helped to shape not only this story, but these characters. I'm so appreciative of the time you took to read and discuss with me.

My family for their encouragement and support. That's you, Daddy (Wally) and best step-mom ever (Kathy).

To everyone above I hope you're holding on tight because I kinda feel like I'm just getting started...

CHAPTER ONE_
HANNAH

HER FILTHY BARE FEET LEFT TRACKS IN THE SOFT DIRT OF THE narrow roadway, but she no longer cared. The hunger drove her to more drastic measures now, often leaving her feeling reckless. A few months ago, she would have kept to the brush line, concealing both her body and her path. But back then she had a reason to stay hidden. Back then she wasn't alone.

With each passing day, as game grew more scarce and the wild roots withered in preparation for winter, Hannah found herself accepting the inevitable. The land was too harsh for her. The lifestyle too unforgiving. But at least she had made it as far as she could. Further than most, whoever they were.

When she died, which she figured would be soon, then she could finally tell Andy she had done better than expected. She could tell him that he had trained her well. It was just the need to keep moving that had done her in. The fact that she could stake no claim, make no permanent shelter. For if she did, the others would find her. And once they had, she would just as soon put a bullet in her own mouth before anything else.

So she followed far behind the group of men that trudged up the road in front of her. Though they didn't know it, she listened to their occasional banter; their rough deep voices stirring a well-earned fear inside her soul.

Their horses too, made noises that frightened her. Their huff of breath, the clop of heavy feet. But she pushed past these reactions, shoving them aside in an effort to survive. Why get so close to them? After everything Andy had warned her about? Well it was simple enough really. It was the food. These men had it.

Each night they would make camp and eat around a fire. A real honest to goodness fire. Laying low in the surrounding trees, her stomach would cramp and ache as the smells of cooking filled the forest. In the morning, after the men had moved on, she would crawl into their camp and eat their burnt leftovers. Tiny bits of meat clinging to half-gnawed pieces of bone. It was delicious. She had abandoned shame a long time ago.

Overhead now a cool breeze blew, shifting the leaves in the surrounding trees. Towering pines, twisting oaks, the occasional cypress, it was thick up here. Tilting her face skyward, Hannah shaded her eyes for a moment, absorbing the fading light from the setting sun. The men had been trekking along at a steady pace, hauling a cart filled with who knew what. She didn't know where they were heading, but the road they were on twisted up and into the mountains, veering perpetually northwest.

Staggering just a little, Hannah was forced to stop and catch her breath. Bending forward, she placed her hands on her shivering bare knees. It wasn't just the cold from having lost her pants that made her shake, it was the exertion of walking itself. Her head swam, alternating between darkness and blinking white light. She was tired, so very tired.

After a beat she forced herself upright and clutched at the pistol wedged into the pocket of her oversized jacket. Well, technically it had been Andy's pistol. He had given her the gun just before... well, she didn't want the scene to play over in her head again, so she wiped it away.

And in the end, it was that exact slip of awareness that cost her. It was Andy's memory, the thing that had happened to him. It made her blind to her surroundings. That and the hunger of course. And the weakness. And the death that hung all around her.

For standing in front of her now, where there had once been an empty road, was a horseman. He had come down from the mountainside, taking cover in the brush where she *should* have been hiding. While her mind was off somewhere else, he stepped out of the thickness, guiding his mount to the middle of the road, where he then stopped and eyed her.

For a single moment, all movement ceased. Hannah couldn't breathe. All she could see was the rider before her. All she could hear was the rush of blood in her ears. But then a shock of fear rushed through her, sending a burst of adrenaline to flood her body. And it only took a split second for her to draw her gun.

She leveled it at him, sitting so high up there on his sturdy gray horse. Between the rise in the road and his position on his mount, Hannah had to angle her arm decidedly up to keep the gun trained on his chest. She felt the strain of the posture in every aching part of her body. She hoped he couldn't see the way she trembled.

For his part, the man only raised his eyebrows, his crystal green eyes registering a touch of surprise. A sweep of chestnut hair peeked out from beneath his faded ball cap and a short beard covered his chin. Though the jeans and navy-blue jacket he wore were decidedly dirty, the black rifle that was slung over his shoulder looked impeccably clean.

Hannah's eyes absorbed all of these details before falling to lock on the pair of tall brown boots that protected his feet. Of all the things that he had and she didn't, she envied his shoes the most.

"I didn't think there were any of you left," he said, shifting slightly in the saddle.

His movement caused his horse to step once, then swish its tail in anticipation. Hannah maintained her aim, hoping the screaming muscles in her arm wouldn't give way before she had a chance to pull the trigger. Andy had told her not to trust any of them. Andy had told her time and again that if it came to this, she had to run. Everything inside of her urged her to do so now. She should be backing away.

But then an inner voice sounded, its tone was one of defeat. How far would she get really? With the man on the horse full of food and water, what were her odds? That answer was easy. Too easy.

But that didn't mean she had to speak to him. And the gun would buy her a few more minutes anyway. A few precious minutes with which to make a final decision.

In the silence, a stillness settled between them, one that seemed to stretch out. His mount became impatient, nervous maybe. She watched as the man slowly uncurled his fingers from the reins and stroked calmly at his horse's shoulder. The man's bright green eyes never left hers as he did it but the beast stilled just the same, then exhaled.

"We thought you were a boy," the man spoke again, but she just blinked at him, trying to make sense of the words. "The size of your tracks were so damn small."

They knew she had been following them, that's what he meant. The realization took its time sinking into her starving brain but once it landed, it hit her like a ton of bricks.

Maybe this was how it was supposed to end, she thought. After the last six months of struggle, she almost welcomed it. Then there came the relief, sudden and all-encompassing. Relief because her inevitable end had finally come. It soaked into her, through her, calming the rush of adrenaline, overriding it.

Her hand holding the gun jumped, then began to visibly

shake. If the man was afraid, he didn't show it. His face remained the picture of calm, he only leaned back a bit in the saddle.

"We've been leaving behind scraps but had I known you were..." he trailed off, biting at his lip a moment. "If I'd of thought for one second that you were a woman, I would've left more. I'm sorry."

They're just words, she reminded herself, no matter how kind they sounded to her ears. But the stress of holding the weapon had become too much. A breath later, her knees gave out.

Dropping like a stone to the road, Hannah felt the impact jar her shins, but somehow managed to keep her arm outstretched. The gun wavered in the air a moment before she righted the barrel to point once more at the man. Her sudden collapse had the horse's nostrils flaring. She watched the great beast's muscles tense, but again the man quietly brushed his fingertips over the gray hide and the horse settled.

Suddenly everything wanted to go blurry on her. Her vision rippled and wavered but she fought hard to keep it clear. Choices, choices. It's time to make a choice.

"You're hungry," the man said gently. "Do you want some food? We'll feed you. I promise no one will hurt you."

Lies. Andy's voice echoed in her mind. *They will always hurt you. There aren't enough of you left, it's made them all crazy.*

But the impulse to give in was coming on strong now.

So very strong. Hannah squeezed her eyes shut against the calling, it was so clear.

Food? Yes, yes she desperately wanted food. And beneath it all, she longed to give up. That's right. A part of her wanted to lower the gun and go with this man. To walk meekly up to him and submit to whatever hell came with it.

On top of that, she wanted so very badly to believe him. She wanted to eat and to feel safe. But the reality of the world she found herself in was that nowhere was safe for her. Nowhere. She had seen that first hand, right? Despite all of the things she could no longer remember, at least she recalled that much.

So with a final push of strength, Hannah opened her eyes wide and sucked in a sharp breath. Jerking back the gun, she pressed it's cold barrel against her own temple. There was only one way to be safe without Andy to protect her, just like he had always said. *Only one way.*

"No, no!" The man spread out his hands, imploring. His horse jumped and danced about. "You're starving to death and you're scared. Maybe you've come across some bad men, but we aren't like them. Please."

For a moment she held his gaze, let her soul reach out and connect with his. There was something about him, if you really took the time to look, she thought, before squeezing her eyes shut and pulling the trigger.

CHAPTER TWO_
COLE

THE CLICK OF THE GUN JAMMING FELT LIKE A PUNCH straight to Cole's chest. Hell, it practically knocked the wind out of him. He kept waiting for the boom, kept waiting for the shot. How many times had he heard a bullet enter a brain? Too many. But the sound never came... because the damn thing never fired.

Leaping off his horse, Cole crossed to the woman's slumped figure before she had a chance to try it again. Yanking the black weapon from her hand, he tossed it behind him before gathering her crumpled body in his arms.

For a split second, he wondered at how tiny she was. But then she began sobbing, great big gasping cries that barely made any noise at all. He could feel her heaving as he drew her further onto his lap, all the while working to keep his grip gentle.

It had been five years since Cole had last held a woman,

three since he'd seen one alive. There were rumors around campfires at night, but that's always only what they were... rumors.

When the war had first come, it had been a brutal one, fast and without warning. Leaving nothing but hollowed cities and death in its wake, it had swept them all up in an instant. One day you were a cocky college kid and the next you were crawling through mud on your belly trying to kill anything in front of you that drew breath.

And it was true the fighting had consumed him. Especially after... well, after what happened with his folks. So shit, he had become good at it. The killing.

So good that it was all he noticed. Too good, really.

It wasn't until the fighting had finally ceased that any of them realized it. But by then it was too late. All the women... *all of them*... were just gone. Not that many men had survived either though, so you could chalk it up to that. And of course those that had survived were changed.

Hell, he was changed too, and not for the better. Which left Cole filled with one burning question among many. Where had this particular woman come from?

Letting his eyes travel down her body, he noted her bare legs were covered in dirt, half-healed scrapes and bruises. Looking closely, he realized how starved she was. The bulky jacket she wore hid the extent of her thinness. Her face was gaunt, with high cheekbones and drawn cheeks. They lacked the ruddy color that belonged there, trading the healthy flush of pink for a sickly sallow. She kept her big brown eyes averted from him, refusing the contact he sought.

What sort of fresh hell had she seen? He didn't want to imagine it.

Ever so carefully, Cole looped one arm beneath her knees and shifted around in an awkward attempt to stand. The effort was made easier due to her weight, or lack thereof, and soon he was on his feet. As he approached his horse, the gelding sidestepped a bit, shying away from the moaning bundle Cole carried.

With a practiced patience he paused, eyeing the gray steadily. After a beat, his horse stood still and let him approach. With his left hand clutching at the saddle horn, Cole used his right to press the woman against him. Thankfully, she didn't resist. He thought she probably lacked the energy to do so.

Placing his boot firmly in the stirrup, Cole hoisted himself and his cargo up, slinging one leg over the other side and settling in. The horse planted his feet and waited while Cole adjusted the rifle on his back and then the woman.

Once done Cole urged his mount forward with a squeeze of his legs. After a few steps, he glanced down at her.

"Here, take this," he said.

Reaching into his jacket pocket, Cole brought out a piece of hard tac and placed it into her palm. It was small, no bigger than his finger, but it was food and a good start. Snatching it from him greedily, the woman pressed the piece to her lips before going completely still. It was like she just realized where she was.

Cole held his breath, but after a moment she took a bite. When he felt her jaw working against his chest, he released his breath with control. She was like a wild animal caught in a cage. Taking food from him was just the first step in gaining her trust.

As their bodies swayed with the gait of the horse, Cole did his best not to stare down at her. She was spooked enough as it was and he didn't want to apply any more pressure. It was hard though, the not looking part.

Lifting his head, he scanned the narrow roadway. The others were just up ahead now. At this pace it would take no more than five minutes to catch them. How would the guys react when they all saw her? Shit. This was the last thing they would expect.

For three days they had known they were being followed. It was in the rustle of brush at night and the sudden too quiet of the forest. Hell, it was in the air. Something that you learned to feel when you spent years being the hunter, and then years more being the hunted.

Half the guys had wanted to search out the culprit but the other half had wanted to leave it be. In the end, Cole's vote had been the deciding factor. He had looped around on day two, doubling back to their camp and discovered the tracks. They looked to be from a boy, maybe about twelve or so. Not wanting to frighten the kid, Cole had gone the long way around to rejoin his crew.

Ever since then, they had left scraps, still debating on

whether to offer shelter to the kid or leave him alone. Feeding themselves was challenging enough and another mouth, that likely couldn't contribute much, left them all debating. When they had finally come to a decision, Cole was sent out to bring the kid in.

Glancing down now at the woman, he watched the flutter of her eyelashes. She still wasn't looking at him. He pursed his lips once but didn't have time to think through what he was about to do. His team was close, just around the next bend.

Letting loose a whistle, long and low, Cole offered a warning of his approach from the rear. He could hear the other horse and the mule, along with some idle chit-chat between Cookie and Trey. Those two rarely stopped talking but upon hearing his call everyone fell silent.

There had been a time when traveling in the open like this would have been a death sentence. But that was before they had earned a reputation for themselves. That was before they had marked their boundaries. Now the team was able to move freely along certain roads at certain times, to conduct raids on the fallen city, or to trade with other groups of men. But the habit of hyper-vigilance was a strong one and their team had fought hard during the war, so if they needed to travel silent, then they could.

"You okay?" Cole murmured. The woman had grown rigid at his whistle. "Like I said, no one will hurt you."

She didn't answer. Cole's stomach churned.

A wind began to gust, causing the leaves in the trees around them to flutter and sigh. The dirt road had narrowed considerably, twisting and turning as it rose higher into the mountains. Beneath him, the gray horse began puffing out his breath, he was eager for the company of his herd mates. Their scent must be on the wind.

Trying to give his horse more leverage for the steep climb, Cole leaned forward in the saddle. At his press of contact, the woman whimpered. Hearing that pitiful sound was like a stab to the gut. She was probably terrified, he realized, a bit too late.

Sitting up, he did his best to shift back and give her more room. This close up though, he couldn't help but look down at her once more. She had a dark mass of tangled hair. Absently, he wondered that it wasn't cut shorter. If she was out on her own with no protection, then at least an attempt at looking like a boy would have been wise.

His thoughts circled back to how exactly she had gotten out here in the first place. How had she survived the war? Where had she come from? Were there others?

"Hey, Boy-o!"

At the sound of Cookie's voice Cole glanced up. The entire lot of them were stopped in the middle of the road. The last bend in the trail had given way and the five other men were spread out in the cautious way that marked everything they did since the end of civilization. Everything they did after the war.

Cookie, the oldest of them, stood front and center. One of his arms was braced against the side of the wooden cart that Davey had fashioned together out of salvage material.

He was handy like that, Davey was, always building something useful.

But the younger man was reserved in his way and so stood in the tree line, blonde hair tucked into a ball cap that was pulled low over blue eyes. He was barely visible at the far edge of the road. Like so many of the others, his fingers itched at the gun tucked into his hip. Cole's eyes swept the rest of his men quickly, noting the way their faces morphed.

The whole lot of them went from curious to downright shocked the moment they really got a look at what he was holding. Cookie's mouth actually dropped open at the sight. The older man with his salt and pepper hair and quick wit was at a loss for words. That might just be a first, Cole thought, working to hide the superior smirk that wanted to play along his lips.

For several moments, no one moved a muscle. The horses each snuffed and stamped in turn but the rest of them were frozen there together, each caught up in his own thoughts, his own memories maybe. Here they all were, the men that time forgot.

And it seemed that several minutes passed, with the wind gently blowing colder all the while. Maybe they would've been stuck there like that forever, if it hadn't been for the woman herself. Turning her head, she looked towards the cart. Cole figured the curiosity at what surrounded her had overcome her fear.

In his arms, he could feel her blinking as she watched the men absorb the sight of her. And Cole was watching them, too. He could see the exact moment that it really sank in. A living, breathing, woman. They weren't all dead. The war hadn't slaughtered them all.

But then the realization seemed to hit them all at once. There was a rush of movement and an explosion of voices. Everyone broke, pushing towards Cole on his horse.

"My Lord," Cookie kept repeating it. "My Lord, I don't believe it."

"Is she hurt?" Questions started coming.

"She looks hungry."

"Where did you find her?"

Snorting a warning, his horse shied away, then began to prance. His steps were high and tight, he was on the edge of bolting. Cole gripped the reins and shifted his legs in a vain attempt at control but then the woman in his arms began to wriggle and turn. She cried out and the noise only made his horse panic all the more.

She was trying like hell to get away. Damn it, he should have anticipated this.

"Easy," he murmured. "Easy."

Fingers working, legs gripping, Cole's eyes shot up and caught the flash of his best friend's dark stare. Positioned on the far side of the group with his raven black hair and broad shoulders, Liam sat astride his bay gelding and frowned.

He was the only one who didn't rush forward, the only one cloaked in coldness. Liam, with his knowing look and annoyed expression. *He* would have seen this coming.

Of course he disapproved, Cole thought. Liam disapproved of pretty much everything. But he was Cole's right hand, his ride or die; the closest thing to a brother you could get without sharing blood.

And hell, they went way back, like waaaay back. The two of them had grown up together when there was such a thing as grade school. So, despite the instant pinch of worry working in his gut, Cole brushed the feeling aside. Liam would come around, Cole told himself, he always did. And anyway, Cole needed him.

THE GIRL CAME ALIVE ALL OF A SUDDEN, SCRATCHING AND clawing up Cole's body like a cat running from a pack of damn dogs. And isn't that exactly what they were to her? A pack of hungry looking dogs. It was like Cole not to see it until the damage was done.

Lips pressed in a firm line, Liam quietly observed the fall out. The woman was scared out of her mind. And if Liam was being honest, he would've felt the same way. Surrounded. There was no worse feeling than being surrounded.

"No hands!" Cole shouted, now. "No hands, boys!"

Liam's horse tensed beneath him, seeming to feel the frustration that oozed from his rider's posture. That, and the swirling mass of chaos on top of the other horse didn't help matters. Grinding his teeth, Liam watched as Cole did his best to stop the momentum.

The gray horse shied away from the rush of men before

prancing in a circle at the commotion on his back. The girl clung to Cole's jacket, burying her frail face in his chest, clutching at him in desperation. Her thin legs that had hung bare over one side of the saddle were straddling it now, but she was facing Cole, trying to make herself disappear.

Huh. Like you could ever unsee the only living woman in three years. Instead, she succeeded in further revealing her lack of pants. Her threadbare underwear made even Liam's gut churn. He looked away, clearing his throat uncomfortably.

The desire to beat the shit out of everyone spiked through his blood stream. And suddenly, Liam had to work to clamp down on the flood of emotion. What the hell was Cole thinking? And where the hell had she come from? Liam rolled his shoulders and huffed a breath as he watched the others back away, all apologies and raised hands. They wouldn't have done a thing to her, except to help, but she didn't know that.

"She alone?" Liam lifted his voice to catch Cole's attention.

"Yeah." Cole glanced up from whispering to her. "But she had a gun. It's back in the middle of the road. There were no other tracks."

"Still. Someone should check, especially now." Liam held Cole's gaze until Cole gave up a nod. The appearance of a woman after so many years was unnerving. She hadn't made it all the way out here by herself.

With a nudge of his legs, Liam leaned forward in the

saddle and guided his mount off the road. He went straight up at first, diving into the thickness of the forest before picking his way south. Mirroring the path of the road, Liam made sure to keep one eye scanning his surroundings. It didn't matter that everything inside him confirmed there were no other people. Instinct or no, he had to make sure.

Liam always felt the presence of men before the rest of the team. Hell, he had been the first to point out they were being followed at all. Call it a sixth sense, or survival instinct. Or maybe it was something worse altogether. Maybe he had just enjoyed being a killer of men far too much in the war. It was a hard habit to give up, one that flowed through his Godforsaken bloodline. Not that he *had* given it up. Because in truth, he hadn't.

The footing on the hillside was steep and crumbling in some places, stealing Liam's attention from the roadway but only for the briefest moment. His gelding was sure-footed, and the horse knew what was expected of him. He, like Liam, was terribly good at his job.

Down on the roadway, the metallic sheen of a gun glinted in the dying rays of the sun. It was small, but anything out of place seemed to give itself away immediately to him. Glancing back over his shoulder, Liam stilled his mount and watched his crew off in the not so far distance. From this vantage point, he could see them coaxing the woman down and into the cart.

Shifting his eyes over, Liam spent a few good minutes surveying the countryside. This was their territory, at least it was the far edge of it. From here on out, they shouldn't have any company, but if the girl was here, then maybe there were others. Not women of course. Liam knew better than that, had seen them killed off, traded and die in the worst of ways. War was a cruel beast that left you feeling sick with all the ugliness.

But if that girl got all the way out here, then she didn't do it by herself. Not for the past five years, anyway. There must have been a man helping her, hiding her, taking care of her. There had to be for her to make it this long.

Liam shifted his gaze back to the weapon and then further down the mountain. His thoughts traveled with his eyes and he figured that if there wasn't any man with her now, then he was likely dead. Because that was what Liam would be, he thought. If Liam had a woman, then he would be dead before he let her out of his sight.

Finally coming to the conclusion that she was indeed traveling alone, Liam urged his mount down through the forest to fetch the gun. Again, caution had him hesitating in the tree line for several minutes before stepping out onto the road to retrieve it. He had seen too many soldiers die from lack of patience. Too many men met their end due to lazy rushing or worse, complacency. Too many women too, for that matter.

His black boots kicked up the slightest dust when he dropped off the side of his horse and crouched next to the weapon in the dirt. He was tall, taller than any of the other men, with dark hair and eyes to match. Quite the contrast to Cole, their fearless leader. The charming one that knew just what to say to get everyone to agree, to get everyone to follow.

And truth be told, Liam was content to follow as well. He didn't like leading. He didn't like the social aspect of it. He preferred for Cole just to point and tell him to kill this one, or that one, and he did so... happily. Not making the decision was a relief for Liam.

Gripping the weapon in his hand, he flicked it open and eyed the chamber. One in, he thought, the damn thing jammed up on her. With quick efficiency, Liam cleared the round and all the rest. All the old revolver needed was a good cleaning and it should be right as rain, he figured.

Quickly now, he stepped up onto his horse and trotted back up the road, throwing a final glance over his shoulder as dusk settled in. So the little spitfire had tried to kill Cole... impressive. For the first time in a long time, Liam suppressed the smallest of smiles.

CHAPTER FOUR_
HANNAH

THE CREAK AND GROAN OF THE WOODEN CART'S WHEELS IS what woke her. She felt dizzy. Dizzy and light and sick all at once. Blinking into the sunshine, Hannah wondered at the time. When she tried to sit up, her head began to spin, and groaning, she lay back down.

The swaying of the cart did not stop. It was a gentle rocking motion, with the occasional bump and lurch that shook her weak body. If Hannah was being honest, it was the most comfortable place she had lain her head as far back as she could remember. Which wasn't all that far, considering.

Squeezing her eyes closed, Hannah raised her hands to her face and sucked in a breath. Try as she might, she still couldn't recall anything past about six months ago. Everything before that was blank and filled in only by what Andy had told her.

Andy. The thought of him made her sick with guilt.

Turning her face into the pile of blankets, she worked to calm her breathing.

"You awake, Little Miss?" A man's voice was close.

Lifting her head, Hannah fought for the second time to open her eyes and adjust to the blinding light. How was it so bright outside? Hadn't she just lain down in the dark?

Slowly, the man's face came into focus. He was older, maybe early fifties, with slightly graying hair and a weathered appearance. He smiled and she felt his expression was genuine. Even though her heart tripped with uncertainty, she realized that physically speaking, she was in no condition to make a run for it.

"Boy-o!" The man called, his head tilting up from his position walking next to the cart. "She's come 'round."

"Thanks, Cookie."

It was the horseman, come alongside her now. His gray horse kept time with the slow moving mule that pulled the cart. She had to shift around to see him properly, bracing one elbow behind her while holding the other hand to shade her eyes.

"Hungry?" He asked.

She nodded slowly, keeping her eyes locked with his.

"Thirsty too, I bet."

Again she nodded, not trusting her voice to speak to him. Did prey dare make a noise in front of its predator? No, prey did not. But the man simply gestured to the one he called Cookie and the cart came to a gradual halt.

Where Hannah wanted for words, the man Cookie

seemed to have them in spades. All at once he filled the silence with a stream of easy chatter.

"Slept the whole night through, did you? We just got all those blankets fresh from the fallen city. Not a cheap trip, if you ask me. How did you get way out here anyway? Do you have any kin? Where've you been living?"

Hannah stared at him for a moment, but then realized he wasn't looking at her while he spoke. Instead, he was fiddling with the harness of the mule and adjusting what appeared to be a brake of some kind on the cart. Before long he was reaching down beside her to retrieve a canvas bag, hoisting it up and over his shoulder. As he walked away towards a small clearing near the road, his voice faded along with him.

Slowly, Hannah pushed herself up to sitting. Her body ached and trembled with the want for food and water, but she did her best to hide the fact. Curling her legs up beneath her, she braced herself against the high side of the cart with both hands. The feel of the smooth wood was perplexing to her touch.

She had never ridden in anything before, nor on anything, as the horseman did. At least, she had no recollection of it. Sucking in a breath she pushed the heel of her hand against her forehead. It throbbed so.

"Would you like help down?" The horseman spoke just behind her, causing Hannah to jump slightly. "Sorry, didn't mean to spook you. Would you rather I brought you food here? You could eat in the cart."

Hannah looked over her shoulder at him, catching the

intensity of his green eyes, and considered. She needed to go to the bathroom, otherwise there wouldn't even be a question of her leaving the cart. A glance down over the side revealed quite a drop. Hannah judged the distance to be about five feet. It was nothing huge for a healthy person to jump, but as unsteady as she felt, she knew she'd need assistance in order not to fall.

Brushing a mass of thick tangles from in front of her face, Hannah let her gaze travel to the clearing where most of the men had collected. As soon as she had, the lot of them looked away.

They had been watching her. It made her gut drop.

She had spent the past months working as hard as she could not to be seen, and to suddenly be appraised by so many eyes at once... well, it had her pulse quickening.

"I'm Cole by the way," the horseman spoke again, drawing her attention back to him, away from the others. "Do you have a name? Can you speak?"

Narrowing her eyes at him, she let the questions play out in her mind. What would it hurt to tell him her name? As she considered, she sucked in her bottom lip and nibbled on it slightly, weighing the level of risk involved. The gray horse stamped at a fly and huffed a breath. Cole stilled him again with the soft stroke of his fingers. The horse at least trusted him, she noted.

"Hannah," she conceded and was rewarded by his crooked smile. She flushed and looked away.

Her voice had come out as a whisper, itchy and dry in her throat. When was the last time she spoke aloud? She had been alone for so long, she couldn't quite recall. Maybe it just felt like a long time; she'd given up keeping track of the days after Andy. He had schooled her time and again not to make unnecessary noise, so after what had happened to him she hadn't allowed herself to speak at all.

"Hannah," Cole repeated.

Stepping down off of his horse, he looped the reins in the crook of his arm before reaching up to her. For a beat, he let his hands hang there in the open space between them, waiting for her to make the next move.

Slowly, her eyes drifted from his face down his arms to stare at his palms. They were callused and rough from hard use but clean, far cleaner than she was at the moment. Uncomfortably, she pushed the blankets off of her and scooted closer to the edge on her knees. She tugged at the end of her jacket, willing it to cover more of her legs than it did.

If Cole noticed, he didn't let on. His hands were still in the air. His eyes blinked patiently at her.

He was frozen in place but carried no tension with him. She had seen him wait on his horse the same way. The realization had her softening so she leaned into his embrace. Without much effort, he wrapped his hands about her waist and pulled her over the side, setting her carefully on the ground.

The chill from the night before still lingered in the dirt and her bare feet absorbed the icy warning of the changing season. It must be late summer, she thought, maybe even fall. Winter would be upon them soon.

Bracing herself against Cole, Hannah took her first few steps cautiously. He kept a grip on her waist, taking one step for every two of her own. Her legs were tingling but they didn't give out and so before too long she pushed gently away from him. It was a test of sorts and after a beat of reluctance, he passed, releasing his hands to fall back to his sides.

The trees were thick along the roadway across from where the others had gathered to sit and eat. Deliberately, Hannah aimed for them and Cole kept pace beside her. Her stomach twisted uncertainly. How was she going to use the bathroom like this?

Upon reaching the edge of the trees, Hannah came to a stop and turned towards him, keeping her face downcast.

"I need..." she whispered it, swallowing audibly in an attempt to strengthen her voice. "Um, some privacy."

"Oh." Cole stood straighter a moment. "Of course."

He turned his back on her then and though she didn't raise her head, she watched his body shift and his boots point in the opposite direction. But that was it, he did not walk away.

After a beat, Hannah realized that was all the space she was going to get. Even Andy, with how close he'd always watched her, left her well enough alone when she had to pee. But Andy was gone now, and she was here with these strange men. The ones she was never supposed to speak to in the first place.

Sighing quietly, Hannah crept up into the woods and found a large tree to hide behind.

CHAPTER FIVE_
LIAM

HE HATED THIS FEELING. HATED IT, HATED IT. THE TEAM WAS exposed, everyone was distracted. This is when people die, Liam thought, grinding his teeth in frustrated silence.

It had been this way the last time. And sure, that was nearly three years ago now, and yes none of their team had gotten hurt, but still. Liam's fingers twitched on the saddle horn as he fought the flood of memories.

They'd been down so far south in the thick of the fighting by then, with buildings burning and soldiers marching. Looking back on it, there hadn't really been anything they could have done differently. By the time they found the abandoned train car, most of the women and children had died of heat stroke anyway.

But there had been that one handful that lasted another few days... suffering. Fuck, he could still see it, still smell it.

Giving his head a sharp shake, Liam narrowed his eyes as Cole dismounted from his gray horse. Even Liam was feeling the slip of awareness now, and the unwelcome fact had his blood boiling. He could not afford this distraction. He could not afford the weakness it brought on.

But then Cole was helping the woman down, and together they were heading for the woods. Liam's pulse ticked up considerably, he couldn't help it.

By the time the girl stopped and whispered whatever it was that made Cole turn around, Liam could practically feel his heart pounding in his throat. She's going to make a run for it. She's going to scream and cry and make all kinds of noise, he thought. But then she simply climbed a few feet into the trees and picked a trunk to squat behind.

She's just going to pee. Because she's a woman and they have manners and all that, Liam realized. His mouth dropped a tiny fraction as the flood of relief hit him full force. So she was planning to stay with them. Shit... he didn't want that, right?

Gritting his teeth against the mix of emotion, Liam let his eyes hop from her hunched form back over to Cole. The fucker was just as jumpy as Liam was. He could tell by the way Cole's hands kept opening wide, then squeezing shut. It was amazing how the woman had only been around for twelve hours and already their entire dynamic was shifting.

Nothing could change a group of men like the addition of a woman. Well... almost nothing. War was pretty good at it, too.

And when the war had started, it'd been unexpected, at least by most. The paranoid preppers faired the best, at least the ones who didn't have a family to look after. The others… well, it was hard to ride out the fighting and fires with a wife and kids. Most didn't make it.

Occasionally now their crew would happen upon a bunker, but the food stores were the only thing left. That, and the bodies. Water ran out too quickly. Water and fresh air, that's what did them in every time.

At the start of the war there had been hundreds of thousands of men fighting. Millions even, judging by the pitiful numbers that now remained. If you ventured down around the cities, or any large waterway, you could still see the evidence all around. Blown out tankers, crashed helicopters, bodies left to rot and decay in the sun.

For the first two years, it seemed the death would go on forever. The strangest thing about it though, was the nukes never dropped. Liam kept waiting for them everyday. They all had. Just end us already, he'd thought, prayed for it even. But when it was all said and done, those bombs never dropped.

Of course by then the fuel had dried up and the ammo, too. There hadn't been anyone working the fields to grow food for far too long. That was the first winter when men began to starve to death.

It had been cold, exceptionally so. The weather was more severe than Liam ever remembered it being. Comfort was rare. Non-existent in fact, so if you couldn't eat, then at least you could huddle around a fire. Maybe the warmth would stop your boots from shaking in the caked-on mud.

But then everything began to burn. Everything and every-one. Well, almost everyone.

There were no cell towers left. No power plants, no electricity, nothing that society had grown so dependent on. The streets overflowed with useless vehicles and the buildings stood empty. Their abandoned hallways were filled with the occasional scent of decay.

How had Liam survived it? How did a man live in a time where only devils walked? Well, you became a devil yourself, naturally. Their entire team, or what was left of it, had been trained for such work. A strike team is what Command had called them.

Hah, Command. They were a bunch of cold-blooded fucking murderers that only birthed more of the same. So Liam and Cole had spent their time slinking around behind enemy lines, hiding for weeks in the dirt. They were hungry, desperate, killing machines, and they'd be doing it still except the orders had stopped coming and Cole had led them north. Liam would be forever grateful for that.

Eyes tracking now, Liam watched the girl get up and return to Cole. His oldest friend went to reach for her but then thought better of it and returned his clenched fist to his side. Liam shook his head. He'd seen that very same man grow into one of the most proficient strike team leaders for the Nor East Side Soldiers. Cole was efficient, focused, driven. He was a damn executioner.

But you'd never know it to look at him now. He was melting into a distracted, uncertain puddle before Liam's very eyes. And where did that leave them? Where did that leave the team? Liam just didn't know the answer and for the first time in a long time he felt a touch of fear.

As he looked on, Cole paced deliberately beside the woman, leading her back to the cart. Still unsteady, she reached up to get in and stumbled back down. Quickly, Cole gripped her waist and hoisted her easily into the cart.

In that briefest of moments, her jacket hitched up again. Liam noted the instant clutch in his own belly and tried like hell to dial back the feeling. He tried to kill it along with so many other things he had successfully killed. If she was for anyone, it certainly wasn't for him.

Swiveling his head, he watched Cole leave her and walk calmly over to the clearing where the others sat. His horse trailed obediently behind him.

It was easy to read the disappointment that rippled through the team as they realized the woman would be staying behind. After all, they wanted a chance to hear her voice, let their eyes play over her face, ask her questions.

But she was still too afraid, so Cole collected up a bit of food and water and carried it back over to her. Liam forced himself to look away then. He forced his eyes to sweep the valley floor that unraveled below them. Someone had to keep watch. Someone had to maintain focus. Lifting his face slightly, he let the wind drift beneath his nose. Nothing.

They weren't far from the compound here, maybe a half day more at this pace and they would be home. At any other time Liam would've already switched out with Ryder or maybe Davey and hunkered down for a bit of rest and food himself. Not today though. Not now.

The others were too distracted. They couldn't keep themselves from looking over at the woman and Cole, who lingered a beat longer than necessary beside the cart. Could they blame him, though? In the same position, would any of them have done different? No.

But Cole was a good leader and the difference was that he *knew* better than to stay. Liam let his lips turn up slightly at the sight of his old friend returning to the clearing with the rest of the crew. Cole wanted to turn around so badly, but he didn't. He even purposefully sat with his back to her. But after a beat he glanced sideways at Liam.

Across the distance, Liam tilted his head to one side and shook it slowly. *Tsk. Tsk. Buddy. What the hell are you going to do now?*

CHAPTER SIX_
COLE

"She asleep?" Trey asked, his auburn hair fell into his hazel eyes and he swiped at it absently.

Cole simply bobbed his head in time with the strides of his horse and let that be his answer. She was the question on everyone's lips and he couldn't fault them, not really. He was as guilty as they were.

Walking together along the last stretch of road, Trey was on foot just beside him, having dropped back from the crew who ranged ahead. Hannah was bundled down in the cart. He had watched her pull the blankets over her head hours ago to shield herself from view. Cole wondered how long she would feel the need to hide.

"I can't wait to see the look on Ace and Chan's faces." Trey let a smile dance across his lips. "They're going to freak."

"Hmm," Cole replied, his mind traveling elsewhere.

Ace and Chan were the last of their team; the ones left

behind to tend to the compound while the others conducted business. All told there were eight men left out of an original squad of twelve. The fallen four hadn't made it through that last mission. The suicide mission.

Cole shook his head a bit to clear it and let his gaze focus on the fence line that ranged out in front of them. It was a mix of materials. Fresh cut wood, salvaged metal, rocks and stone. But it served its purpose.

That had been the first order of business almost three years ago when they'd selected this spot. They needed the fence to keep the livestock in, give them room to graze and roam. It was high up on top of the mountain, had flat areas that could be easily cleared, and running water. Not a lot of water, but enough.

Coming up to the gate now, Cole could hear a low whistle emanate from somewhere in front of him. The answering cat call from Ace was enough to crack the tension that always came from returning home, wondering what you might find.

In front of them the rusted metal gate swung open, pushed by Chan whose short stature belied the deathly quickness with which he could fight. His short crop of black hair was rarely tucked beneath a hat. He'd once confided to Cole that he didn't like how it made his face look more round than it already was. Cole had laughed back then, not realizing how rarely Chan spoke of such things.

It was back when the war had first started and they were all eager to do their part. Back when they were young, so young and naive in so many ways. What would he give to go back to being twenty-six, with all the others calling him old man?

Nah, Cole shook his head again. It wasn't the number of the years, it was the feeling of inexperience that he missed. The innocence of not knowing. When you'd never held a brother in your arms and watched the life leak out of his eyes. He wanted to go back there, but back there was gone.

"Boy-o!" Cookie called out to him in his usual way.

He was the oldest of them by far at fifty-two but he had no problems keeping up. He'd been placed in their unit for one reason and one reason only. He was an expert sniper, a damn crack shot and the best Cole had ever seen.

His real name was Lawrence Smelt, but he went by Cookie almost immediately. The one rule he insisted on was that he handle the food, and the rest of them had readily agreed. *It makes their faces go away*, he'd told Cole. *The cooking does.* And Cole knew exactly what he meant. The faces of Cookie's kills were on an almost constant repeat in his mind, and the activity made it stop.

Refocusing on what was in front of him, Cole saw the reason for Cookie's shout. The cart hadn't even made it halfway through the gate before Ryder spilled it about the woman. Ace and Chan had rolled their eyes in disbelief, not wanting to fall for whatever prank was about to be unleashed on them.

Eager to prove himself truthful, Ryder, the youngest of them, stepped up to the side of the cart and pulled down on the blankets. For the briefest moment, Hannah lay still, apparently deep in slumber. But the moment the chill evening air brushed against her, she woke with a yelp.

Scrambling back, her bare legs kicking out sporadically, she wedged herself into the furthest corner of the cart. Cole could practically feel her shaking inside his own body.

For their part, Ace and Chan stood in wonder, mouths agape, saying nothing. Why was Ryder such a dumbass? Cole fought the flash of anger that wanted to dominate him as he urged his horse forward. But he wasn't fast enough.

By the time Cole came to a stop at the cart, Liam was already there, yanking Ryder down by the collar of his shirt and laying him flat in the dirt.

"No fucking touching," Liam spat. His voice was scary empty, the way it usually was.

Everyone froze. But then as quickly as he had taken action, Liam stopped. He righted himself on his horse and took his reins in hand. Calmly, he shifted his eyes to find Cole. The message he was transmitting was so typically Liam that Cole received it, loud and clear.

This is your problem. Do not make it my problem. Cole could practically hear his old friend say the words before he whirled his horse around and trotted further into the compound. It was everything Cole could do not to roll his eyes.

"I didn't mean anything by it." Ryder stood, brushing dust from his shoulders.

The kid respected the hell out of Liam, and was half

scared of him, too. If Cole was being honest, so was most of the team. But they didn't know him like Cole did. They didn't know him from before.

"It's been a long ride," Cole said to everyone and no one in particular. "Let's all get in and settled."

As the others grumbled in agreement and poured though the gate, Cole dismounted and let his green eyes find Hannah's brown ones. Reaching in, he grabbed the blanket she'd been under and tossed it to her. When her hands snaked out to take it, he let out a quiet sigh. How exactly was he going to handle this?

As she covered herself back up, Cookie pulled on the mule to get the wheels rolling again. Normally, Cole would trot out to the far shed alongside Liam and tend to his horse before releasing him out to graze. But now he wasn't entirely sure he could let Hannah out of his sight.

She was too vulnerable, and he didn't just mean physically. Only yesterday he'd watched her try to shoot herself in the head. He couldn't live with himself if she actually succeeded the next time. There could be no more dead women, no more dead children. Not on his watch.

Hell, Cole thought, she just might be the last one alive in the whole world for all he knew.

Looking back over his shoulder, Cole noted Trey still keeping pace with him, though a few feet to one side. Turning to the other man, Cole handed over the reins and nodded.

"I need you to clean him up and turn him out for me."

"Will do, Boss." Trey chanced one more peek at the cart before striding away.

The compound itself was nothing fancy. In the dying light Cole surveyed his surroundings as if seeing it again through new eyes, through her eyes. Once inside the fence, there was a wide swath of trees they used as a natural sight barrier. The narrow dirt road that led through the gate squeezed through the thick trees before it opened onto clear land.

To his right were a series of small buildings, all wood, cut with axes and built with their bare hands. To his left the mountain continued to climb ever so slightly, with trees dotting along the incline for stability. A few of the men had positioned their tiny cabins up there, preferring the protection of cover to flat ground.

If you kept pushing past all of that, there was a stream that ran along the length of the compound and the lower pasture. It provided enough water for all of them. They were even able to keep a few sheep and a goat.

Coming to a stop in front of their largest structure, Cookie let loose an audible sigh as the mule brayed. The building itself was used primarily for storage, though it wasn't more than twelve feet wide by twenty-four feet long. Inside, wooden shelves were posted up on the walls and filled with canned food, extra clothing, blankets, you name it. They'd even dug a cellar in the floor and lined the walls with stone.

Directly across from the storeroom was a large fire ring with half hewn logs spread around for seating. It was the team's gathering place. It's where they ate in fair weather and cooked meals in the warmer months, although it wasn't so comfortable during winter. But no worries there, Cole had big plans for improvement. Cole always had big plans.

As soon as the cart stopped, Cookie began his typical chatter. Methodically, he unhooked the mule, making sure to replace each strap of the harness just so. The animal groaned and shook its long head. Every so often, Cookie's fingers would find an itchy spot on the brown hide and pause to scratch. You could hear the huff of appreciation from the mule. It was that gentle sound that finally brought a tentative smile to crease Hannah's lips.

Cole knew he should be helping to unload. He should be issuing orders and organizing materials. But instead he was fixed there in place. Watching *her*. Watching Hannah.

CHAPTER SEVEN_
HANNAH

"THE GUYS ARE GOING TO UNLOAD THE CART NOW," COLE spoke, his eyes boring into her intently. "You may want to climb out."

Nodding, Hannah pushed herself up from the corner of the cart and glanced about before deciding to reach for him. The way he quickly stepped to her and held her waist had her swallowing. She would need to be careful.

With both feet planted in the dirt, Hannah stepped back as the other men approached. Turning her head, she let her eyes drift over her surroundings. Darkness was steadily falling now and it was getting harder to see.

The building in front of her was the biggest she had ever seen. Blinking, she squeezed her eyes shut and ran through her mind hopefully. At least it was the largest one she could remember seeing.

All of her time spent with Andy had been in low slung shelters of fallen tree limbs and dried pine needles. They'd never taken the time to actually build anything. Of course that didn't mean larger buildings weren't out there. Something inside her figured there were, but despite that, she couldn't bring one to mind.

Now that she thought about it, the only other building she'd seen was that one in the night. The one with the strange material that looked rough and gray. It was definitely nothing she had seen in nature, close to rock, but not. There was a word for it, she felt certain. *Concrete.*

It came to her in an instant. Now how would she know that? She had no memory of seeing anything like it before. Flashing back, her pulse jumped and her throat tightened. That place was a bad place, and she never would have gone close if Andy had still been with her.

Stepping further away from the cart, Hannah clutched absently at her throat and forced herself to open her eyes. *You aren't there anymore. You aren't listening to the crying.*

Eyes tracking, she caught Cole's stare and quickly lowered her arms to her sides. This place could easily turn into that place. Though here she had been fed, given water and warmth. Despite the swirl of men all around her, passing back and forth from the cart to the building, no one touched her.

They looked at her though, but with smiling faces. Smiling, all of them. Well, all except for the one, but he wasn't here now. He had gone off on his brown horse.

He didn't like her, she could feel it. The way he furrowed his brow, with his dark eyes assessing. Now that was a predator if she ever saw one. And she had, back with

Andy. The hunters and the killers, they all had that same look about them. That same energy. Something that made you stop in your tracks, your insides curling tight, your heart picking up steadily.

Though her mind refused to reach further back than half a year, Hannah could remember everything since then clear as a bell. Back then she hadn't been quite so hungry all the time and she had pants and boots and a thick sleeping bag at night. It had been just after dusk, almost the same time it was now. Andy had her crawling low on her belly in the leaves just behind him.

They had tracked the paw prints all day long, up the side of the mountain and down to the wide stream. It was there they had seen the carefully hidden den, the push of dirt, the awkward bend to the surrounding branches of a bush. Andy got his bow out, he never used the gun for game. *It's too loud, never use it on anything but a man*, he had said.

And there they waited. Waited until her neck was stiff and sore. Waited until she had to lay her cheek to the ground just to get some relief. But finally the wolf came out, with his mottled gray coat and his lips curled in a snarl, revealing whitish-yellow teeth.

He had come towards them then, he wasn't afraid. And while Andy rose to a knee, bow drawn back in a split second, the wolf's eyes zeroed in on Hannah.

Something in them was flashing. Flashing with a spark she would later realize was intelligence. But then Andy had killed him, and they had eaten their bellies full for a week.

The meat had tasted so good to her at the time. She could still recall the slip of grease along her fingers.

"Hey, you okay?"

Hannah glanced up, her eyes clearing from the scene in her head, and was taken aback by Cole standing just in front of her. Nodding her head slowly, she ran her hands along the sleeves of her jacket and held back a shiver that wanted to crawl up her spine.

It was thoughts of Andy that kept her slipping. She wondered how he would feel about that. He'd always been so adamant about her awareness. *Focus Hannah, keep your eyes always looking around.*

But then at night his tune would change. *What are you thinking about? Don't you remember me? I'm in there somewhere. You love me, Hannah, you've always loved me.* When she would shake her head no, his response was always the same. A sad sort of smile would creep across his face before he pulled her in to kiss him. And she let him. Because she had loved him, right? At least that's what he always said.

"Looked like you were off somewhere," Cole continued, his eyes shifting across her face.

"No," Hannah lied, glancing down at her toes.

"The fire's started." Cole gestured behind her before going on. "And Cookie is going to make dinner. Do you want to sit with everyone?"

Looking over her shoulder, Hannah watched the half-circle of faces in the dancing light from the flames. It was pitch dark now. The stars were out but there was no moon. How long had she been standing there staring off? A lot longer than was normal, she was afraid. Why was it so hard for her to stay in the present?

Sucking in a breath, she turned back to Cole, wringing her hands tightly in front of her. Her stomach growled unhappily as her mind traded ideas back and forth. They wanted her to sit with them but she didn't want to get any closer. Fires and men were definitely off limits. The smoke gave away your location and the men... well, they did what men do.

But she was hungry. So incredibly hungry, and they had all behaved well enough thus far. Was it enough to chance the flames? After a beat, Hannah bobbed her head in acceptance and let Cole lead her on.

Eyes darting covertly as she approached, Hannah counted the lot of them. Eight. There were eight men altogether, including Cole who took a seat on one long split log. He sat on the flat side which was facing up. With the rounded side down, the seat rocked a bit on the uneven ground as he settled himself.

Just to one side, the man called Cookie leaned over a metal grate that was propped up amidst the flames of the fire pit. In his hand, he held a long wooden spoon. Glancing over at her, he gave her a quick nod just before returning to stir the contents of a large black pot. Whatever was inside of it smelled like heaven on earth. Saliva collected unbidden inside her mouth.

Nibbling at her lip, Hannah hitched up the blanket she had wound about her waist and sidestepped a log before settling down on the one beside Cole. The others murmured in greeting and she let herself meet a few of their eyes before refocusing on the fire.

The dark-eyed man was sitting further back than the rest but she noticed him straight away. His presence radiated out to her and she couldn't help but feel his stare like a hot brand against her skin. *He doesn't approve of you. He doesn't like you here.*

Shifting in place next to her, Cole drew her awareness to him once more, though he didn't reach out or touch her. Keeping her eyes downcast, Hannah listened as an awkward silence began. It would have settled in permanently, she was sure, had it not been for Cookie. The older man began a steady string of dialogue that seemed mostly aimed towards another man he called Trey.

The two of them bantered back and forth for a few minutes, easing the tension until the others joined in as well. Hannah listened carefully as they discussed their successful trip to the city. She'd never seen the city herself, though Andy had described it to her. He had been adamant she should never ever go near it. There were still many men living inside its abandoned buildings, dangerous men that wouldn't think twice before hurting her. Maybe she should have listened to him more. If she had, would he still be alive?

"I still think the price was too high," grumbled Cookie.

"We needed the tarps before winter," Cole reminded

him. "They knew how badly we wanted them and that affected the price."

"Still." Cookie turned his back on them and rummaged through a small box. "Three of Liam's knives was too many."

Hannah quickly scanned the group and watched a few of the men glance back at the dark-eyed one, who kept an impassive face. Liam, so that was his name. Without a hat to cover his head, Hannah noticed the blackness of his hair that so matched the color of his eyes. From the smooth olive-color of his skin to his high cheekbones and hard jaw, his looks mirrored the intensity with which he carried himself.

He certainly drew attention. Commanded it in fact. Hannah let herself look a few moments longer than she should. He didn't have a beard like so many of the others. But then his eyes shifted to meet hers and her stomach flipped. He caught her watching him.

Heat flooded her cheeks as she dipped her head, cowering instinctively. If she could melt away right now, she would. At any other time she would have simply run. But there was no running here. Not when you were behind a high fence, in the midst of the trees, surrounded by buildings and men.

Tilting her head to the side, she looked first to Cole and then past him to Cookie. At least those two men were safe. Yes, they were both safe she decided and exhaled.

When nothing more happened, Hannah forced herself to tune back in to what was going on around her. Cookie's voice droned continually. He kept complaining about the trade deal to the encouragement of some and the teasing of others. They liked him. They all liked him a lot and she could see why.

Smiling at the realization, Hannah watched his movements. Beside him, in the flickering light of the flames, sat a series of cans. Hannah could see pictures of food on them, though their mostly white labels were worn and torn in places.

Chili beans, black beans and yellow corn. As she stared hard at the cans of corn her heart rate accelerated. Inside her chest, a whirling tightness grew. Then her eyes were squeezing themselves shut as her mind exploded with a sharp bright pain. And when she opened them again, she wasn't at the fire anymore.

Her hands rested on the twin doors of a small metal cabinet. The silver handles were cool beneath her palms but the room itself was warm. Glancing over her shoulder, Hannah noted the man sitting with his back to her. Like always, he was hunched over his desk, scribbling notes on a pad of paper then lifting his head to blink at the large computer screen before him.

Turning back to the cabinet, she twisted the handles and pulled the doors open easily. With a light laugh, she reached in and gripped a can of yellow corn. Turning the pristine label over in her hand she felt a smile of amusement fill her face.

"Why do you still keep these Dr. B?" She asked.

Rotating around, Hannah waved the can side to side in the

air as the man swiveled in his black office chair. Behind his thick glasses, she could see his eyebrows lift in surprise before he cleared his throat uncomfortably.

Uh-oh, she thought, her breath stilled in her lungs, I've done something wrong.

But the doctor merely lifted his shoulders and gave his head a quick shake, sending his brown mop of hair to sway. He's trying to play it off, Hannah realized as she watched him steal a glance at the camera positioned in the upper corner of the room.

The light blinked as it always did, a watchful, continual red.

"Oh." Hannah exhaled the word in a rush before her eyes shot wide.

The memory. It was her very first from before Andy and it was over too soon. The doctor and the room were gone. She was back sitting around a fire at night, surrounded by men she didn't know. It had been so real. The images had sparked so vividly inside of her that she began to shake.

Leaping from her seat on the log, Hannah dove for the can of corn and clutched it in both hands. She could hear the surprise in the men around her, could feel them watching and moving, but she didn't have time to focus on that. With every fiber of her being she squeezed the can tightly and willed her mind to go back there. She willed herself to go back, to remember everything. She wanted more, so much more.

But try as she might, the experience wouldn't go any

further. The vision wouldn't go beyond what it had revealed before. There was just the doctor and the desk and the camera. The blinking red camera, but nothing else.

When she closed her eyes, murmuring to herself, she could only see what she had already seen. *Who are you? We knew each other. Where was that? How can I get back there?*

Tears leaked from the corners of her eyes and she could feel herself begin to break down. The murmurs of the men had grown louder and when she finally looked up, she saw the concern that covered their faces. Half of them were standing.

Cole, as usual, was crouching beside her, reaching out. She felt the moment his fingers brushed her elbow.

"You can have it." Cole nodded to the can in her hands. "The whole thing if you want."

"She's just hungry."

"She's crazy."

"Wouldn't you be?"

"Shut up."

The other voices raised around her, arguing over her display. And it hit her how she must look to them. The blanket lay discarded in the dirt, she swayed on her bare knees, thin legs sticking out of an oversized filthy jacket. Her hair was a tangled mess and her bony fingers were still wrapped so tightly around the can that her knuckles had turned white.

She did look crazy, completely insane in fact and perhaps she was.

They didn't know that her mind was a frustratingly

blank abyss that had only now given up its first glimpse of the truth. They didn't know what it was like to not know who you were, or why you seemed to know the names of things but couldn't bring them to mind.

Purposefully she loosened her grip and set the can shakily back on the small crate. Looking up at Cookie, he merely gave her a nod with a pitying sort of smile on his face.

"It's almost done, Little Miss," Cookie said. "You'll be the first to get a bowl full."

"I- I-" Hannah stuttered, her eyes darting around to them. "I'm sorry."

CHAPTER EIGHT_
COLE

IT TOOK EVERY OUNCE OF STRENGTH COLE HAD NOT TO PICK Hannah up right then and carry her away. Watching her unravel over a solitary can of corn steeped him in guilt. He was an asshole, no doubt about that. What the hell had he been thinking? He knew she was hungry, knew it from the thinness of her face and the way her hands shook.

But he told himself you couldn't give a starving person a ton of food right away, so he'd been controlling her portions. Now he regretted it. Was she really so desperate for a little more? He felt cruel and stingy.

When Hannah finally composed herself and they sat back down together, Cole wanted to cover her hand with his own, but he didn't. The others were all there. And Liam, with his anger brewing, was watching. He knew what his friend was thinking, too. And the kicker of it was, Liam was probably right.

This woman was going to be the end of their life here together, at least how it was now. They were already arguing about her. Arguing about her food, her lack of clothes and where she would sleep. But the thing of it was, Hannah didn't seem to notice. She didn't hardly seem to hear them at all.

Something was off with her, but Cole couldn't quite place it. Then again, it had been many years since he'd spent this much time with a woman. Maybe he'd just forgotten how it was.

"Here ya go, Boy-o." Cookie handed him a small bowl of the chili, but was looking past him. "It's for her."

"Thank you," Hannah whispered as she accepted it.

She was careful to take the bowl with soft hands as Cole passed it over. And that must have been hard to do, considering that it smelled so rich with steam lifting from the rim. Cole's mouth watered along with everyone else's.

Normally they ate pretty well, all things considered. But the corn and chili beans? That was something rare. Apparently Cookie had deemed this a special occasion because they hadn't come by those cans easily. No, no. They had killed for them in fact. Literally murdered otherwise innocent men.

Then with cold and careful calculation, they had stockpiled all of the items in their storage building alongside everything else that men were willing to die for. And there were an awful lot of those types of things these days.

So, pulling out the cans of corn and bag of white rice was a luxury that didn't come along all that often. When it did, it was usually reserved for the dead of winter, when spirits were low. Because its not like there was a canning factory up the street that could duplicate what was in front of them. Once it was opened and eaten, it was gone forever.

Gone forever, like everything important. Gone like women, like electricity and grocery stores and hot running water. Gone like cars that drove down roads and planes that flew through the air. Gone like the four other members of their team, dead on a mission gone terribly south. That was when Cole had first looked up. Like really looked up and around.

And what he'd seen back then had frightened him. Scared him so fucking bad that he'd decided right then and there to end it. That was when the orders from Command had "stopped." Cole made the decision to defect, and the others followed; some knowing more, some knowing less.

But then on their march north they found the train car. After that came the dead bodies lying all around and the heaps of mass graves. Women's mass graves. You could tell by the clothing, by the hair and the shoes. And by the tiny kids beside them and under them.

It made Cole sick to think of it, even now. And not much made his stomach turn anymore. It was just the children. That and what their team had done later. What it had taken for them to survive. What they'd done at that farmhouse.

As more chili was passed around, shining silver spoons began to dip greedily into blue porcelain bowls.

Glancing down at his own hand, Cole twirled the etched metal spoon around in his fingers. It had come from that farmhouse, too. The dishes, the silverware, the cooking pot.

Cole let himself remember. He let his mind go back there to when his team had first come through the area. It was still wild at the time. Wild and unclaimed. The massive fires that were sweeping the south hadn't made it this far north and even before that the land had been rural and tough.

When their team found the compound, with its flowing water and the possibility of sustaining life, they had decided to stay. But they weren't the only men around. No, there were others.

Men who had dodged the draft, were too old, or too young. There were even a handful of other defectors, though not in such great a number. It had taken a fair amount of brutality to build their place. And a fair more amount of killing to keep it.

By that time though, the team had been bad men for so long, what did it really matter? What was offing a few more men when you'd already annihilated more than you could count? So they had. Frequently. Indifferently.

But then there were times when you'd still feel it... the killing. There were times when no amount of familiarity could cure you from your conscience and that little voice inside you would suddenly start talking again, telling you how wrong you were. But then again, you couldn't quite hear it over the sound of your own stomach. And so the farmhouse had been just that. It had been all of that and more.

They'd discovered it in the spring. Cole had been on a scouting mission with Liam for a little over five days. They had trekked east, cresting first one craggy mountain and then the next. Occasionally they came across paved roads but they never followed along them, only crossed over them, keeping instead to the forest.

They were on foot. It was back before the horses, before the sheep and the mule, too. And they were hungry. Very hungry, which made them finally decide that the risk of encountering men might be worth the reward.

Back-tracking to a paved road, they followed its path, hiking just above it until it split. Veering to the right, they kept moving until they came across a gravel driveway. It was night by that time, and the darkness made them feel safe.

The land was rocky that high up, with fewer flat spots carved out of the mountainside. By the time they reached the end of the road, a clearing had appeared and at the bottom sat a two-story green house with a red painted roof.

Like Christmas, Liam had murmured.

They lay on their bellies, side by side, noses barely above the dirt, watching from a few hundred yards out. At first it all seemed so surreal. The house was untouched, with full glass windows glinting in the reflection from the moon. No lights were on, no fire, no lamp. But they had seen some awful ambushes in their time, their last mission being no exception, so they waited. They waited with patience.

After a while, small details began to creep out at them. The steps were clean, someone must have swept them. No cobwebs clung to the eaves, a person still dusted them away. Then the wildlife got used to their existence. The animal sounds began, and with them the stamp of hooves, the sigh of livestock. Cole turned his head ever so slightly, looking sideways at Liam who knew what was on his mind before he even spoke.

We'll need everyone, Liam had whispered. *I'll stay here and keep eyes on. Try to find out how many there are and where.*

Cole had nodded then, his muscles tight with tension. Whoever had managed to keep this place for this long in this condition was no one to mess with. It could be a blood bath.

But by then he'd already seen the glint in Liam's eyes, had shared it even. The rush of it all was a pounding of blood in his ears that became a steady roar. They would take what was here. They would conquer this place.

And after a month long siege and five dead men... they had.

"She's falling asleep," someone commented, and Cole glanced over at Hannah.

Her bowl was empty but still clutched in her left hand, the spoon was dangling from the fingertips of her right.

Leaning forward, he caught a glimpse of her soft face as it tilted forward, her chin nearly touching her chest. Sure enough, her eyes were half-closed.

Shaking her shoulder gently, Cole called her name and she roused.

"Where's she going to sleep?" Trey asked, not able to quite keep the hope from his voice.

"Where do you think?" Cole shot him a look before remembering he needed to keep the peace. "I'll be on the floor, so keep your mind out of the gutter."

The others chuckled, and the tension eased.

Standing, Hannah let him guide her by the elbow and together they walked away from the fire. Cole's cabin was small, about twelve foot square, and centrally located just past the storage building. It wasn't where he would have preferred to have it. In all honesty, he would have liked to hide way up in the tree line like Liam or Davey. But he didn't have that luxury. He needed to be accessible at all times.

There was always someone that needed him, for an opinion, or a helping hand, to solve a conflict or discuss a problem. And for the most part, he was happy to do it. He loved his guys, everyone of them, to his core. He would give them his life if he had to. Hell, he had tried.

But he wouldn't give them Hannah, he thought suddenly, and the realization made him uncomfortable.

"Wait here," he told her, and pushed open his front door.

It was dark inside but he knew every inch of the space

by heart. He walked a few steps forward, then turned to the right and crouched at the pile of kindling he always left sitting in his makeshift fireplace.

Pulling the knife and flint from his pocket, he struck quickly along the strip and caused sparks to jump in the blackness. The tinder bundle ignited and he blew carefully, with control, until smoke poured forth. Shoving the bundle further under the small twigs and larger split logs, he sat back. It would take.

Glancing up to the doorway, he watched her silhouette framed on the threshold. The low fire wasn't big enough to illuminate her face yet, so he couldn't tell what she was thinking. He could only assume she was nervous by the set of her shoulders and the way she gathered her jacket closer around her.

"You can have the bed." He gestured behind him, to the twin mattress that lay on a low wooden platform in the corner. "I'll grab my bedroll from the cart and sleep on the floor."

When she didn't answer him, he stood up and took a survey of the space. It was sparse, a bachelor's existence, with a handmade wooden chair for sitting and an old dresser for his clothes. The wall above the bed had a single window, one taken from that farmhouse so long ago. It opened even, if he wanted.

It was home to him and comfortable enough, but nothing like what she was probably used to. There were no curtains, no pillows, no rugs to cushion the wood floor. No knickknacks or keepsakes to line the dresser. That item too, had been taken from the farmhouse.

"It's not much, I know." He looked over his shoulder at her, then back to the room. "But the mattress is clean, we got a bunch of them from..." he swallowed, then thought better of his sentence, "from a while ago."

"It's a bed," she said, the awe clear in her voice. "A bed."

Cole stepped back as she brushed past him. In the dance of growing firelight, he watched the way she ran her fingertips over the worn quilt that he'd thrown over the mattress. Rubbing his hand over the back of his neck, he wondered at her reaction. It was almost like she'd never seen one before.

"Yeah." Cole let the smile that wanted to play on his lips come out. "It should warm up plenty in here and I'll grab you another blanket. You could keep the jacket on if you want, or I could give you one of my shirts to sleep in. Maybe a pair of my boxers would fit you, too."

"Are you sure?"

"About the bed or the clothes?"

"Both."

"Yeah, I'm sure." He bobbed his head and crossed to his dresser.

Pulling open a top drawer, he dug around until he found the smallest pair of boxer-briefs he had and then the softest shirt. After sliding the drawer closed, he brought the items to her and set them on the bed.

"Thank you," she whispered, before letting her eyes drift up to his.

A genuine smile creased her lips and Cole felt his whole body go taut with it. All he could do was bob his head again and then push his way outside. When he closed the door behind him, he leaned back against it for a moment. He had to keep his hands off of her, he had to.

CHAPTER NINE_
LIAM

CROUCHING DOWN IN THE PASTURE, LIAM RAN HIS HANDS through the grass. Judging by the color, it would hold over for at least another two months. The dirt beneath it was rich, it rained often enough up here to keep things alive.

Around him, the tiny herd of shaggy white sheep munched and grunted. There were only six of them but the one ram was doing his job. Just last year they'd gotten two new lambs.

Standing, he let his gaze follow the gentle slope of the hill until it met with the creek that ran year round at the bottom edge of the property. Each day was growing steadily colder, with the sun dropping down earlier and earlier all the time. If Liam had to guess, he would say it was around late September, but the names of months and when they occurred were a thing of the past.

For certain it was fall. The leaves on the trees that were not evergreen had begun their change. A few of the maples that dotted the hill around his cabin were already showing yellows. Soon enough there would be oranges and bright reds.

It was pretty. He huffed a breath, rolling a piece of plucked grass between his lips absently. What did he care about pretty?

Still. It had a certain feel to it, the way the earth kept going despite the best efforts of its human population.

"How're they looking?" Cookie asked. The old man had walked down from his precious storage building under the guise of talking sheep, but Liam knew better.

The moment Cookie crested the fence to the pasture, Liam had sensed him. The sheep had paused in their crunching, lifting their noses, licking at the wind. Out of the corner of his eye, Liam had watched the man come on, stomping and clomping the way he liked to do when they were safe on the inside of their little wall.

Cookie enjoyed pretending they were normal again. It was a habit that got under Liam's skin, though he couldn't say for certain the reason. Maybe everything got under his skin now. But the old sniper was quick enough otherwise, so Liam would let it slide, or try to.

"Good," Liam answered finally.

"We'll want another one in the next few weeks."

"Will it need to last all winter?"

"That'd be nice."

"The one lamb is bigger than the other, but it's female," Liam spoke aloud, but mostly to himself. "I'd prefer to take the male, we won't need him."

"There's eight of us to feed," Cookie reminded him.

"Nine, you mean."

"She's small."

Liam pursed his lips and remained silent. Yes, she was small. And that was what the old man had really come to talk about. The girl, not the food supply. But Liam wasn't about to let him get his way that easy. So he turned his attention back to the herd and eyed them appraisingly.

"I could take the one that didn't produce a lamb last year," Liam gestured. "She's fat enough, and that would give the male a chance to grow another season. We could slaughter him next winter."

"Sounds like a good plan."

Bobbing his head, Liam glanced up at the sun and judged the time to be a bit past noon. Lunch had probably already been served, with him down with the animals. But Liam didn't mind missing a meal. Often he preferred to take his bit and go off alone. Cookie usually saved him something, or brought it down.

Hopefully, Liam glanced back at the older man, but saw no small bundle.

"You missed lunch," Cookie pointed out, following Liam's train of thought.

"I guess so." Liam paused. "What was it?"

"You're avoiding her."

"I went to dinner last night."

"And took breakfast early this morning," Cookie countered. "What don't you like about her?"

"Nothing."

"He's going to keep her," Cookie reasoned. "He'll need your support."

And that was the heart of the matter, wasn't it? Liam pinched the bridge of his nose and closed his eyes. Cookie was paving the way, as usual, helping to quietly keep the group together by keeping Cole at the head.

It was like this with any major dispute, any major issue. Cookie worked the crowd slowly and methodically. Lurking behind the scenes he used his non-threatening manner to get into everyone's head. Then he would work both ends to the middle and whisper information in Cole's ear.

It was necessary, Liam knew, and helpful. In the past he himself had been grateful to the old man on more than one occasion. They all had. They all wanted Cole to stay where he was, none of them wanted the burden he carried.

"What are the others saying?" Liam asked, looking up.

Cookie shrugged, then added, "they all want her to stay."

"You mean they all want her."

"They'll get over it."

"No. They won't," Liam corrected. "They'll all leave."

Again, Cookie shrugged before commenting, "maybe a compromise could be reached... sometime in the future."

"You're scheming," Liam observed.

"Either way-" Cookie let a knowing smile play across his lips as he patted Liam on the back. "He'll need you."

"Speaking of which..." Liam let his eyes pop up to the high fence line once more. "Here he comes now."

And just behind Cole, like a little shadow, walked the figure of the girl. She kept her face downcast, focusing on the steps that Cole was taking. Her thick tangle of greasy hair fell forward over her shoulders. The oversized man's t-shirt she was wearing swayed with her body as she walked. It was one of Cole's shirts, Liam recognized it immediately.

With the sun at its highest point, the temperature was probably in the seventies. It was a nice day, sure enough. Liam's eyes tracked down to her bare legs and the pair of men's boxer shorts that hung low around her waist. Despite his best intentions, his blood began to warm, he couldn't help it.

Clenching his jaw purposefully, Liam glanced away.

"If you can't say something nice..." Cookie murmured, and had Liam rolling his eyes.

CHAPTER TEN_
HANNAH

SHE HAD FOLLOWED COLE. FOLLOWED HIM OUT THE DOOR to breakfast, then wandered behind him as he spoke to Davey about a new building they were planning. She kept a few steps back as he walked and occasionally he turned to look at her, but he didn't say anything. He didn't tell her to stop, so she kept on going.

If she had discovered anything over the past few days, it was that Cole was safe, relatively so. He was respected by all the men he came into contact with and so she figured if she stayed within his line of sight, then she would be safe by extension.

He chatted with Chan, who was Asian, though the word had come to Hannah without much thought. And also with Ace, who had creamy dark skin and big brown eyes. They discussed the upper fence line and how it could use reinforcement, then walked to survey a few trees that Ace wanted to cut down for the material.

While the men talked, Hannah wandered over to a collection of large rocks and sat. The rocks were warm from the sunshine and she drew her knees to her chest before resting her chin on them. Absently, she let her hand drift down to pick at the lines of white crystal that cut through the gray stone. It was nice here, all calm and orderly.

Lifting her head, Hannah surveyed the buildings that dotted the clearing down below them, then the pasture that stretched out beyond that. All morning she'd thought about that can of corn and her memory of the doctor. If only there was some way to make it happen again.

She knew there were supplies in the longest building, the one right next to Cole's cabin, but she hadn't been inside of it. Maybe if she could get her hands on more things, things like that can, then more memories would come to her.

"Alright guys," Cole was saying. "Why don't you start on these trees and I'll get Trey to come up and help you."

"Sounds good, Cole."

"Thanks, man."

Hannah looked up in time to watch Cole end his conversation and move back down the hillside. As he passed her, she rose to standing, brushing her hands on the large shirt she wore before moving to follow. Though he didn't glance back over his shoulder at her, she knew by the way he slowed his steps that he wanted her with him. He placed his boots carefully, almost deliberately showing her where the best spot was for her next step. It had been that way with Andy, he had wanted her close.

She frowned at the thought of him, and the things he used to tell her. About how she should never let another man see her, and if she ever got caught that she should find a way to run as soon as possible. If Andy were here, he would want her to leave this place.

But if Hannah was being honest with herself, she did not want to leave. This was the safest, most secure home she had ever known. She had to have lived somewhere else before, but Andy had said the war wiped everything out. So if there was no Andy, and no home from before, then why not stay here? Where else would she go?

"It's a nice day," Cole said, breaking into her thoughts.

"Yes," Hannah agreed, keeping pace behind him.

"In another few hours, it will be even warmer out."

They had reached the flat dirt just behind the fire ring and he paused, looking left and then right, searching for something. Hannah stopped as well, but had eyes only for the storeroom, wondering what it might hold.

"Would you like to clean up?" Cole resumed walking, having found what he was looking for in the distance.

"What?"

"After lunch." Cole sidestepped an overgrown bush, then started up a narrow trail that cut diagonally along the hill. "It will be hot enough to swim in the creek. You could wash if you want."

Hannah came to a sudden stop, but then quickly rushed

forward in an attempt to keep up with him. "You mean like with soap?"

"Yeah." Cole threw her a crooked smile over his shoulder. "We even have some shampoo tucked away, I think."

"Shampoo," Hannah repeated the word, rolling it around on her tongue strangely.

Nothing leapt readily to mind. Soap though, that she definitely missed. At first Andy had a whole bar of it and they had bathed in streams and small ponds every chance they got. But after a few months, the bar dwindled to nothing.

Come to think of it, she didn't know where it had come from originally. She hadn't ever thought to ask how to make more. Not until after it was too late, and he wasn't there to answer.

"I would like to," she said finally.

"Then you will."

After lunch Cole stopped at the storage shed and went inside alone. When Hannah tried to follow him, he motioned for her to wait. Twisting her hands together she leaned forward, trying to get a peek beyond the threshold, but was unable to see around the half shut door. He emerged moments later with a towel tossed over one shoulder and a faded blue canvas bag.

"Ready?" He asked.

The grin that painted his face was charming, she realized, her eyebrows shooting up briefly in response. Turning, he walked a few paces ahead of her, but then stilled.

"I'd like for you to walk next to me," he said finally. "You don't have to follow behind."

"Alright," she said, but felt uncomfortable all the while.

With Andy, they had always traveled single file, always. He led the way, and she kept her head on a swivel behind him. In that fashion, he was the first to encounter any obstacle, the first to be attacked, the first to defend. She watched his flanks, and occasionally the rear. It was a good rule to live by, and live by it they did.

So to be next to Cole, with his confident stride and easy demeanor, was unsettling. It wasn't until they crossed into the pasture, opening the wooden gate, then closing it behind them, that she drifted back to her comfort position.

Below them, she saw the two men standing amongst the fluffy white animals. Their bleating and grazing was disturbed only briefly by the newcomers approach. Sheep, she thought. They're called sheep and you can eat them.

Squeezing her eyes closed, she pushed her mind forward. Feeling fuzzy images shifting somewhere in the background, she was unable to bring any to mind. The sheep before her were the only ones she could remember seeing.

"How's the feed?" Cole was the first to speak, Hannah came to a halt just behind him.

"Should last another two months, maybe more," Liam answered.

"Did we harvest enough this summer?" Cole again.

"It'll be close," Liam answered. "But I think we'll be able to swing it. The tarps we traded for should make all the difference."

"Worth three of your blades?"

"Definitely," Liam conceded, while Cookie grumbled unhappily. "I spread them over the stacks this morning. Should keep everything high and dry."

"Perfect." Cole glanced back at Hannah, then returned his gaze to the other men. "We were just going to the creek. Hannah wants to wash."

An awkward silence ensued in which Hannah swore she could feel all their eyes resting on her. She kept her focus on the wispy blades of grass at her feet. The ones that blew causally in the soft breeze before coming back upright.

"Well, we'll just scoot along then," Cookie spoke up. "Give you a bit of privacy."

If she hadn't glanced up just then, Hannah would have missed the elbow the older man delivered to Liam's side. It was a quick jab, and another man may have cried out, or at least exhaled, but Liam didn't budge. His eyes were on her and their focused scrutiny was more than she was used to. Another time she would have looked away, but something about him trapped her there, pinning her to the spot.

"Of course." Liam ducked his head finally, breaking the stare before moving off.

It wasn't until they were a few steps up the hill that Hannah inhaled fresh air. She hadn't been able to breathe with his eyes on her like that.

"Don't worry about him." Cole grabbed for her hand and tugged on it. "The creek's just down this way, you can see it from here."

Hannah let herself be led by him, feeling the way his hand held onto her own. Warmth crept up her arm from his steady touch. It was unlike anything she had experienced.

Before she could get too wrapt up in the strangeness, she heard the gurgle and flow of running water. As the hillside dipped down to meet the tree line, there was a depression in the earth, and in it ran the stream.

It sparkled in the light from the sun, sending rays to bounce into her eyes so she had to shade them with her free hand. Her filthy dirty free hand. Suddenly, she found herself eager for this. Eager for the chance to get clean, wash away all the bad that had coated her. And it was so very much bad.

At the water's edge, Cole stopped and almost reluctantly, he let go of her hand. Setting down the towel, he opened the bag and produced a white bar of soap along with a peach-colored bottle of shampoo.

"I'll turn my back and promise I won't look." Cole handed over the items. "But if it's okay with you, I'd like to stay here until you're finished."

"Yes," Hannah answered quickly, her words coming out in a rush. "I don't want you to leave me."

Cole smiled at that, his vibrant green eyes played over her a moment before he bobbed his head and turned around. Hannah sucked in a breath and stared at the objects in her hands. She knew it was crazy for her to be so attached to Cole's presence already, knew that he was really still only a stranger to her. But for some reason that stranger had become a lifeline.

He hadn't hurt her the way Andy had described. Instead, she was given luxuries she hadn't even known she wanted. And she wanted them. The bed and the blankets. The food and the soap. The clean clothes.

Above all else though, he made her feel protected. She didn't want to be the starving haunted girl he had found only two days previous. Not anymore.

Rotating the bottle of shampoo in her hands she read the words printed across its curved surface. In spots the letters were rubbed away, but she got the gist, it was for your hair. *Of course, shampoo was for your hair*. And there was something called conditioner, too. But dang it, that was all she had in her.

Shrugging her shoulders in frustration, she set the soap and bottle on the grassy bank of the creek and stripped out of her clothes. Cole's clothes, they smelled like him. Putting a testing toe in the water, she found it to be icy cold.

Breath hitching, she stepped down into the stream and sunk up to her knees. Water was always so shocking, she thought, why did it have to be so cold? With a determined grimace, she splashed the rest of the way in and sunk to her neck. The creek was fairly shallow, about four feet deep in the center, so she crouched in the flow and let her skin become numb.

When she was properly immune to the intense cold, she held her breath and dunked her head all the way under, then pushed back up, sputtering. It felt good. She could feel the dirt loosening from her already.

Making her way back to the side of the bank, she looked up at Cole who still had his back to her. She blinked at him awhile before reaching for the shampoo and beginning a good lather against her scalp. The suds grew and grew under her touch until she dunked back under, only to begin again.

"You okay?" Cole called, the next time she surfaced.

"Yeah." Hannah huffed a breath before grabbing the bar of soap. "It's just cold."

"I was thinking," Cole talked with his head held at an angle, not looking back at her, but so she could hear him better. "Davey is pretty handy with stuff and maybe I could ask him if we could carve out some kind of tub. It'd probably end up being pretty small but if we hauled a few buckets of water, we could heat them on the fire and you could have a hot bath. Not all the time, but sometimes. Would you like that?"

"A bath."

"Not a big one."

"You'd make the water warm… for me."

"Yeah."

"It sounds amazing."

CHAPTER ELEVEN_
COLE

"She's got marks all down her back." Cole paced, running his hands through his mass of chestnut hair.

"Like tattoos?" Liam watched him, leaning against a towering pine in the dark.

"No, they aren't tattoos."

Shit, he wished they were tattoos. If that's all they were then he wouldn't feel so fucking nervous. Cole had waited until Hannah fell asleep before leaving her in his cabin to go seek out his best friend. Now the two of them were positioned on the hillside. The fire just below them still had a few of the crew lingering over their dinner but if they kept their voices low, no one would hear a thing.

Pausing, Cole glanced down to his cabin. He knew no one would approach it now, but even so, he kept the door within his line of sight. Watching out of his peripheral vision, Cole resumed his pacing once more. Some loose dirt and rocks tumbled thoughtlessly down the hillside.

"Like scars?" Liam ventured, frowning. "Did someone beat her?"

"No, it was like writing. I wasn't that close and it was only for a split second."

Cole stopped to fight the sickening feeling that threatened to take over. He had recognized the marks well enough, he just wasn't prepared to admit it. Not out loud. Not yet.

Hannah had been bathing in the creek and Cole had told her he wouldn't look. For the first ten minutes, he had been able to keep his word, but then he just couldn't help himself. Before he knew it, he was glancing over his shoulder and thankfully her back had been to him at the time.

She didn't see him do it, but Cole saw the marks imprinted on her spine and it sent a chill through him. Whirling back around, he'd had to work hard to calm himself down. He didn't want her to know what he'd done. He didn't want to violate the trust he'd been working to build with her.

"Did you ask her about it?"

"No, I didn't." Cole stared at his friend, then hissed. "What do you want me to say? Hey, I can't control myself and I'm just a pervert after all and was trying to see you naked, but saw all this fucked up shit on your body instead."

"Alright-" Liam held up his hands. "Alright, I get it."

"Shit."

"What do you want to do?"

"There was only the one set of tracks, right?" Cole dropped his hands to his sides and stepped closer to Liam, letting his words come out low. "She wasn't with anyone?"

"She was alone," Liam confirmed with the slightest nod. "I checked."

"The gun, was it anything special?"

"No." Liam shook his head easily, but his shoulders gave away his tension. "Run of the mill revolver, it just needed cleaning. You got lucky."

"Me?" Cole huffed a laugh then glanced away. "She wasn't aiming at me."

"What?"

"Never mind."

"Tell me." Liam's voice was calm, but uncompromising.

They didn't keep secrets from one another, not since they'd been six-years-old and Liam had shown up to school with a black eye. That had started Liam's first confession to him. And of course, Cole had run and told his parents all about it and then CPS hadn't been far behind. That's when they'd discovered all that terrible mess with Liam's mom.

Swearing under his breath now, Cole held his hand up to his head with two fingers pointing at his temple and pulled an imaginary trigger. Liam's eyes widened a second in surprise before clouding over.

"Happy?" Cole resumed his pacing, his mind a swirl of other, more important things.

"No." Liam gritted his teeth. "Want me to do a sweep?

All access points… the lower mountain? I could cross into the valley and maybe even ask around."

"Yes to the sweep, no to the valley." Cole shook his head. "I don't want anyone thinking we may have found a woman, or even someone new. Avoid all contact, but if you can't, then keep your lips sealed."

"That's never been an issue for me," Liam pointed out. "I'll leave before first light."

"You should take someone."

"Chan? Ace?"

"Ryder," Cole offered. "He could use the distraction. He needs to get out more. How long will you be gone? When should I come looking?"

"Five days." Liam shrugged. "Maybe seven at the most."

"Good."

Cole turned to stare down at his cabin door. It was still safely shut. The inside was dark with just a touch of smoke emanating from the pipe they had rigged up as a chimney.

Silence settled between them, and it wasn't unpleasant. It felt natural, a comforting familiarity after so many decades together. Cole knew that Liam didn't like her coming, and he knew sending his friend out on this errand probably grated on his nerves, but he needed him. Needed him bad.

"And Liam," Cole murmured just before his friend turned to leave. "Don't get yourself killed or anything. I can't do this without you."

Liam answered him with a slow nod before retreating

up the hillside. He was heading to his cabin, and Cole would have to do the same.

After waiting a beat, Cole sucked in a breath and picked his way carefully down to the flattened clearing and then back to his front door. Placing his wide palm flat on the heavy wooden surface, he pushed ever so slowly inward. The faint scraping of the bottom edge against the flooring made him cringe but there was no getting around it. He made a mental note to file it down in the morning.

Once inside, he closed the door behind him and then stood still, letting his eyes adjust to the dim light. The fire he'd started for her had burned low, but it still managed to provide a touch of illumination. A sliver of moon had appeared where there wasn't one before. Through the window above the bed, Cole could see her body.

For several minutes, he watched the gentle rise and fall of her breathing. She was asleep, he was certain. On the floor lay his bedroll just where he had left it. A gentlemen would simply undress and crawl back into it, but he hadn't been a gentleman in so very long.

Sidestepping the sleeping bag, he approached the mattress as his heart began tapping out a rapid pace. Years of training and experience had him controlling his breathing, forcing his mind to stay alert and responsive while his body calmed.

Slowly, he crouched down so that he was eye level with her. She was lying flat on her belly, her head turned away from him, towards the wall. The mass of hair that he'd originally thought was dark lay smoothly brushed and scattered on the pillow. Ace had supplied the brush. Who knew the man had been hoarding like five combs? Anyway, after Hannah had washed the dirt out and let it dry in the sun, her hair had turned this golden honey color. It was silky and long, and a part of him itched to touch it now, but he didn't.

Looping his fingers under the edge of the blankets he lifted them up a few inches before waiting. When she didn't stir, he carefully pulled them down to her waist. The shirt she wore, his shirt, was already hitched up a bit from her sleeping. His boxers were loose but managed to cling to her thin hips. The food she had eaten in the past few days alone had already started the return of color to her once pallid skin. Within a few weeks, she should gain enough weight to hide her ribs.

Looking at her now, sleeping so peacefully, he waged an internal war. She was beautiful. Too damn beautiful.

A part of him, the old human part, knew how wrong it was to be doing this. He should stop right now and go lay back down on the floor. But the other part of him, the soldier, had to have answers.

Because the marks that ran the length of her spine? The ones that were made up of tiny dashes and dots, the ones with long thin lines that interchanged with thicker blocks. They were familiar to him. Oh so fucking familiar. It made his blood run cold.

How many times had he seen that code? How many times had the little blips come up on Chan's scanner?

Giving them orders for another mission, another person to assassinate, another building to bomb.

Originally, Cole had not been trained in the language. It was a secret code that Command used in their communications. That had been Chan's specialty. His scanner would beep, he would read out the marks and Cole would execute.

But over time, Chan had taught him. He schooled Cole in the meaning and implications of each collection of marks. *What if something happens to me?* Chan had reasoned. *You could carry on the missions. Make this whole thing stop.*

Because that had been all of their hope really. If they could kill enough "bad guys," if they could shut down the opposition, then couldn't they all just go home? But then there was that last mission. The one where Cole couldn't quite believe what he read. And the feeling in his gut had been so heavy, so damn heavy.

They were down south aways, like a long ways. It had been months since they had slipped past the main fighting line. There were no uniforms at that point, no real difference in the way the enemy looked and the way they did.

So traveling back then hadn't been too much of an issue. For sure you avoided groups of men. But if you happened to be caught in the open, simply marching in a line and nodding your head at whoever passed seemed to be enough.

It was two years in, and the supplies on both sides were running low. Food was becoming scarce, not to mention fresh water and ammo. Everyone was dirty, filthy and tired, so fucking unbearably tired. Troops were thin and so far down, well, no one actually seemed to know what they were doing.

Cole happened upon a burned out suburb and they hunkered down in one of the two-story houses. It had been pretty once, you could tell children had lived there by the scattering of toys in a few of the rooms.

In the attic, they found a few cans of food, something stashed by an owner who had later fled. Or maybe the man had gone off to war while his wife and kids... well, no one really could say for sure where they had gone. Though later Cole discovered a few old graves in the backyard. Two of them were pretty small. Too small.

Cole and the crew were in the upstairs master bedroom. His back was leaned up against one wall while some of the others slept. Chan was in the adjacent bathroom, throwing up in the toilet that no longer flushed. He had already seen the orders by then, but hadn't come to Cole with the information, yet.

In the far distance, they could hear the pass of a jet, then the shake of a bomb hitting the ground. So many bombs had rained down that this one barely stirred them. Could this one be the nuke? Finally?

Nope. No such luck.

Cole had seen the satellite images about six months before. They hadn't been sent down south yet and he'd been sitting in a tent positioned in a hollowed out factory in a destroyed city. His superior, one of many anonymous faces in Command, had been making a phone call. Holding the thick sat phone up to his ear, the guy paced. They didn't use names. None of them ever gave him a name. It was for their protection, of course.

So while the officer was busy, Cole waited, and for quite a long time, too. In the corner though, just behind a rickety table that was serving as a desk, was a small television. It flashed videos of death and destruction, and Cole absorbed it with marked fascination.

Every major city, all over the world, they were all flattened. Bodies were stacked in the streets, along riverbanks, in deserts... burning. Civilization was gone. Long freaking gone.

Liam had rolled over on the bed then, his too long legs made it so that even on a king sized mattress his feet dropped off the end. Groaning, his old friend woke and sat up, rubbing a hand down his face. Chan returned from the bathroom and something about him was off, but then again that wasn't so unusual, considering their circumstances.

Later that night, when the only thing that hung in the sky was the moon, Chan had described the orders for their next mission.

Cole had blown out a quiet breath as Chan whispered the instructions to him. The building in question was a damn fortress. Guarded on every side, by every sort of combination of man, weaponry and technology, it housed the opposition's leader and he was the target. Kill the enemy's commander, that was the mission.

Maybe that will end it, he'd said to Chan finally. *If we can do it, maybe it will all end*. But then Chan had looked him in the eye, really fucking looked. After a beat, his hands trembling, he shoved his scanner beneath Cole's nose and told him to read the last part. The last part of the order.

Once target has been neutralized, proceed to terminate as follows:
Cole S. Tanner
He is a double agent. Then assume point position and return to Command. Over.

Well son of a bitch. Cole blinked. Turns out *he* was also part of the mission. Chan had been ordered to execute him, too.

And the shit show that followed? If Cole could take it all back, then he absolutely would.

So what he was about to do now? In his very own cabin? Putting his hands where they certainly did not have any permission to be?

Well, it was just par for the course really. The soldier in him would not be denied. So Cole pushed down on his conscience and pulled up on Hannah's shirt.

CHAPTER TWELVE_
HANNAH

She heard him. Well, she heard the scraping of the door opening really, but she kept her breathing even and her body perfectly still.

For several minutes, she felt him watching her. It was so long that she thought maybe he had already laid down on the floor, he was just that quiet. But then he was moving and everything in her body quivered when he knelt beside her.

She could hear his controlled breathing, just barely audible above the thunderous beating of her own heart. It took all of her will power, all of her self-control, not to jump out of her skin when he pulled the blankets down around her waist. Suddenly she was the prey again, with the predator hovering so very close.

Keeping her breath even, she stilled, like a bird trying like hell to blend in so the bobcat that's coming can't see you. Then Cole was lifting up her shirt, slowly, very agonizingly slow. And she felt his fingers trace whisper soft circles against her skin. His light touch ran up her spine, sending a scattering of goosebumps to populate her back.

Her heart raced. Thumping and pumping, it pushed blood to her toes as her belly clenched. Then a heat bloomed in her core, causing tingles to spread somewhere deep inside. It wasn't something she had felt before, and the aching had her wondering.

When his fingers left her skin, he pulled her shirt back down to cover her completely. Before she knew what to think, he had returned the blankets up to her shoulders and left her side.

Silence.

He must have lain back down on the ground but she dare not turn to look. She dare not open her eyes. What had just happened? She didn't know, and part of it frightened her, and part of it didn't.

Sleep did not come easily back to her. She wasn't sure if it ever would.

CHAPTER THIRTEEN_
LIAM

HE'D BEEN BACK FOR SEVERAL WEEKS AND COLE STILL hadn't confided in him. Though he knew something was bothering his friend, Liam wasn't one to push the subject. When Cole was ready, he'd come around.

Until then, Liam sat at his workbench smoothing a file over the edge of the new knife he was working on. Seeking out imperfections, he worked with patience, head bent, eyes narrowed. Of all the activities, this one was the only thing that soothed him.

When he sat in his four by six shed, with the door hanging open and the wind cruising through the open slotted window, his mind quieted and he felt the tiniest hint of peace.

He had built the shed next to his cabin, tucked between large maples and the thick trunks of pines. From the doorway, he could look down and just see the fire ring between the trees. It was a good vantage point, one where he could work in silence but still track the comings and goings of the crew.

In front of him, he had hung an old shelving unit taken from that farmhouse they had raided. He kept various tools positioned just so, easy to reach as he sat on his stool. A box to his left had chunks of metal piled in it. He had every type and thickness, from a mound of old horse shoes to pieces of car parts he had hacked off and then melted down.

On the wall to his left, he hung all of his finished blades, and anything else he was working on. It took a long time to construct the perfect knife. But he enjoyed the skill involved, and of course he enjoyed using them. Maybe too much. A small smirk played across his lips. Yeah, a little too much.

His sweep of the mountain hadn't revealed a thing out of place. There were no fresh tracks made by men, only the game trails and sign he was used to seeing when hunting. That didn't mean he hadn't hiked the shit out of Ryder though.

Spending that much time with the kid one on one reminded Liam just how young he really was. Ryder couldn't have been much more than seventeen when the war started. At night, laying tucked under a rocky over-hang or beneath a stack of brush, Liam listened to him talk and talk and talk.

He had whispered at least, so Liam didn't tell him to shut it. For some reason, Ryder just needed the conversation. Well, actually it was a pretty one-sided conversation.

Liam merely grunted on occasion when the need would arise.

The kid had gone on about all the women he had been with, so many women. But the stories he would tell, well... it had Liam wondering if there had ever even been one. It was quite possible the kid was a virgin. And that was a sad sort of thing to realize because, what did they say? It was better to have loved and lost, than never to have loved at all. Something like that.

But on the other hand, Hannah's presence wasn't quite the same level of torture for Ryder as it was for the rest of them. For Ryder, it brought on yearnings of things he had never experienced, but for the rest... well, they knew exactly what they were missing. And that was a shitty, shitty feeling.

Liam huffed a breath and paused in his filing. He gave the blade a toss and flipped it a few times in his hand, wanting to gauge the balance of it. A knife, no matter how sharp, wasn't worth a shit unless it sat perfect in your hand. Rolling his shoulders, Liam's ears picked up the shuffle of leaves further down the hill. Someone was coming.

He didn't bother to turn his head, but instead returned to his filing. And who could this be?

"Hey, Liam," Cole's voice called out when he drew close.

"Hey," Liam answered.

Shifting around on his stool to look out the door, Liam watched his friend come to a stop before he tucked his hands in the front pockets of his jeans. Behind him was his little shadow, she never left his side. Liam's brow furrowed when he spied her, knowing she was the reason Cole was so twisted up lately. Him and everyone else.

And it wasn't like God had gifted them with a properly plain girl either, one that would be easier to ignore. No such luck there. Nope, Hannah was hot. Like actually hot. Her body had filled out over the past month of steady nutrition. Her hair was clean and shimmering and thick, and her big round doe-brown eyes just cut right into you.

Liam pinned her with his gaze, watching her squirm until she finally looked down. Her lips pouted just a little. It had his nerves pumping.

"I've been wondering if you had a knife that would fit Hannah," Cole said, ignoring the tension. "Something small."

"For her?" Liam's eyes darted to Cole who rolled his eyes.

"Yeah man, for her."

"What for?"

"What do you mean what for?" The laugh Cole released was incredulous. "To cut stuff, to carry, same as everyone else here."

For a moment, Liam's mouth hung open in shock. Then just as quickly, he dialed himself back in and pushed off of his stool. Two short steps brought him further into his shed where he let his eyes travel over the selection of blades he kept hanging on the wall.

He made all kinds. Some for hunting, for gutting and cleaning game. Then others for rougher work, when you had to build fence or cut line. Eyes scanning, he reached out and stroked his fingers along the sharpest knives, the ones that worked best when you had to murder a man, or men. Stopping short, his hand lingered over one.

The handle was a stained wood that he had agonized over to get smooth. It was flashy, and small, easily concealed in your belt, or boot. Selecting it, he felt the weight in his hand, ran his thumb over the red-tinted handle. It would suit her.

"This one," Liam announced.

Turning on his heel, he crossed to the threshold of the door and pushed his way outside. The little shadow was wringing her hands in front of her, eyes bouncing from Cole's face to Liam's then to the ground. In that moment, she seemed too frail to him, too delicate. As pretty as the knife, but not nearly as sharp.

He reached out his hand, the blade balancing in his large palm. When Cole went to grab it, Liam moved his hand away, eyes dancing to his friend as a warning.

"Let her take it," Liam murmured. "Not that she knows how to use it."

Cautiously, the little shadow lifted her head and shuffled her bare feet towards him. Coming in close, she pressed her body into his space, wrapping her slender fingers around the hilt of the knife. It was closer than she'd ever been to him and he was forced to look down on the top of her head. He could smell the scent of her and his body seemed to tense all at once, reacting to it.

Then suddenly she closed the last tiny space between

them, her entire body pushing tightly against his, one small hand snaking out to grab his belt. Liam's lips parted in shock as her other hand came around and stabbed quickly at his back.

Once, twice, three times.

It was in such rapid succession that she was done and releasing him before he even had a chance to push her away.

Stumbling a bit, Liam felt the place on his lower back where she had landed the blows, just over his kidney. It would have been a slow, painful bleed, but she had hit him with the handle of the knife as opposed to the blade. She never even broke the skin. It was a warning.

The little fucking spitfire could use a blade, Liam realized. She could use it well. Her eyes danced at him then and a knowing smile creased those pretty lips.

"Thank you," she said quietly before turning to head back down the hill.

Still stunned, Liam held his hand up in front of his face, awed by the fact there was no blood there. Cole's laugh echoed all around him, then. When Liam shifted his gaze to look, Cole was doubled over, tears leaking from the corners of his eyes.

"Ha, ha, very funny," Liam said, his voice still a bit unsteady. "I hope she lets you make it through another night."

CHAPTER FOURTEEN_
HANNAH

SHE SHOULDN'T HAVE DONE IT. SHE SHOULDN'T HAVE stabbed him that way. Well... fake stabbed, but still. It was the sneer on his face when he said she couldn't handle the knife, that's what did something to her.

Well, actually it was Liam that did something to her. In the moment she'd pressed herself again him, her body had heated and her belly clenched. The feeling lingered even now, though she told herself it was just anger. Yes, she was just upset, that was all. Just frustrated at her lack of composure.

Stomping down the hillside, Hannah kept the knife rotating and rotating in her hand. It felt good. The handle was smooth and fit comfortably in her palm.

By the time she got to the fire pit, the tingling in her body had eased and she took a moment to really look at the blade. It was beautiful, with a swirling red-tinted wood handle that felt soft to her touch. Running her finger carefully across the metal, she noted the sharpness of the edge, the clean pure lines. Liam was an artist, she realized, truly.

The knife Andy had given her was nothing like this. It had been a little too big for her, and flipped open when you pressed a small metal button. The handle had been a dark green and made of plastic, a heavy-duty sort of plastic that had raised bumps for a grip.

She couldn't count how many times she had used it to help him skin the animals they killed, or cut up the meat. On more than one occasion, she had suggested he use it to cut off her hair, or maybe he could cut it with his own, sharper knife. But he had never let her do it.

Always, Andy ran his hands through her locks before bringing them to his lips. *Never cut this*, he would whisper before moving his lips from her hair to her face.

"Quite a show you put on back there." Cole had come around to face her. His smile was big, making his crystal green eyes sparkle in amusement. "Who taught you to do that?"

"Andy," Hannah admitted, the word was out before she knew it.

"Andy," Cole repeated. "Was that who you were with? Before?"

Hannah nodded then swallowed hard and looked back down at the knife. She hadn't meant to give Cole a name. She hadn't meant to ever tell him anything. She'd successfully dodged all of the questions he'd asked up to this point. But he had a way about him, Cole did. A charm that had you relaxing, easing into your surroundings.

She'd witnessed him use it on half the guys here at one time or another over the past month. They came to him with an issue, or an argument, and he would listen, nodding and rubbing at the scruff of beard on his chin. It was the listening, the patient understanding that did it. He made you feel like he really wanted to know the whole story. He made you feel like you were being seen, being heard, that you counted.

"He was," Hannah finally answered, careful to only give him a little bit more.

"Will you tell me about him?" Cole ventured. Easing a step closer, he let his hand brush the hair off her shoulder. "We could go for a walk."

When she looked up at him, his eyes were tracing over her face, gauging her reaction. He had an intensity to him that she couldn't deny, but it wasn't forceful in any way. If she had refused to tell him more, then he wouldn't have pushed it, he wouldn't have gotten angry or stormed off.

And maybe that was why she suddenly felt the pull to confide in him. He deserved it, didn't he? To have the information that he wanted from her? Because he hadn't asked for anything else, he'd only given things to her. And so she owed him... in a way.

Nibbling at her lip a moment she nodded her head and let him take her by the hand. Quietly, they walked off together towards the pasture and the creek beyond. All the while, he let his thumb brush over the back of her hand. The gesture had a warmth spreading itself inside her chest. She could trust Cole, at least with this much.

"We had been doing well," Hannah began, focusing on the soft wrap of Cole's palm on her own. "There were lots of rabbits around and Andy was good with his bow so we didn't get hungry that often. The thing of it was, he didn't like to stay in one place for long. We never had a cabin like you, or a wall, or anything."

"Wait." Cole glanced at her. "You spent the past five years without a home? No cabin? No house?"

Hannah shrugged at that, not able to answer it fully. She could only really speak to the past six or seven months, that was all she could remember. But she wasn't ready to tell him that her mind was blank. She wasn't sure what his reaction would be and deep down she thought that it meant something was wrong with her. Like really wrong, because Andy had always told her so. She wasn't right in the head.

"Sorry," Cole said finally. "Please, go on."

"So we had to move, we had to leave. Andy was very particular about how we traveled. He liked to walk early in the morning or right around dusk, sometimes even in the night if the moon was full. If there was even a hint of other men, then we would have to go back, find another way."

"Andy was your boyfriend?"

"Husband," Hannah said, repeating what Andy himself had told her over and over.

The thing of it was, she couldn't remember getting married, though he had described it to her many times. She had been in a white dress, he was in a tux, which was a black sort of jacket with pants that matched. They had been in a church and promised to belong only to each other. And she was his wife so she had to do things with him, things that he liked.

"I see," Cole said quietly. "So he taught you how to defend yourself with a knife? What happened to it?"

"Yes, he showed me how to use a knife," Hannah confirmed, thinking back on it. "And we had lots of things with us back then. We each had a backpack with sleeping bags that tied on the top. I had other clothes and a pair of boots even, with socks."

She looked down at her bare feet, already so dirty from walking around. Cole had searched for a pair of boots that would fit her, but they were all so very big that it was useless.

Sighing at the thought, she lifted her eyes to the wooden fence that bordered the pasture. Beyond it, the horses grazed together and the mule brayed, making a strange sort of squealing sound. The sheep were out of sight, likely up in the trees somewhere.

Stopping at the gate Cole went to open it, but Hannah stilled his hand. She didn't want to go further, not today. Leaning on the top rung of the fence, Hannah pointed to the creek so small down below and went on with her story.

"We came to a river," Hannah said, she could see it in her mind now. "It was so wide, with the water rushing past. It makes the creek down there look like nothing in comparison. For days, we walked along the shore, hoping the water would slow or there would be a place to cross."

"But there wasn't one," Cole supplied, and Hannah nodded.

"No, we would have to swim across."

"Can you swim?"

"Yes," Hannah confirmed. "But Andy was careful. He always liked to go on ahead, to make sure everything was safe. The other bank was higher, with tall grass that covered the edge and trees that cropped up past that. We agreed he would swim first, and check it out, then he would wave me over."

"Could he swim?"

"Yes." Hannah smiled at the memory, Andy really could swim well. "He didn't think I could make it with my backpack, so I stripped off my boots and tied them to it, then he took both bags and went across. I watched him go. He was like a fish, cutting through the water. It was really nothing to him."

"So he made it to the other side."

"He did. I watched him stand up and toss the backpacks into the tall grass. Then he turned and waved me on. So I got into the water and started to swim. It was so cold and fast and my jacket was heavy when it soaked through. He had left me with the gun just in case, so I held it above my head, but I could barely keep my face above the water. My jeans were soaked too and it only got harder to swim."

"You were sinking."

"I was, but I could have made it." Hannah gulped at what came next. Squeezing her eyes shut a moment, she could still hear Andy screaming at her. "The thing was,

106

Andy didn't think so. He started to yell at me. He told me to take off my jeans, told me to take off my jacket."

"That's how you lost your pants?"

"Yes, but his yelling... it attracted attention."

"Men?"

"They came out of the grass, there were three." Hannah shook her head once. "No, four maybe. And I watched him put his hands in the air. He never looked back at me, he didn't want them to see me in the water."

"What did you do?"

"I kept swimming, trying to make it over to him, but then they forced him to kneel. One put a gun to his head... and when I saw the blood spray out, I stopped swimming."

Cole stepped to her as her face crumpled with the memory. Wrapping her up in his tight embrace, he murmured comforting things into her hair. Turning her face to the side, Hannah pressed her cheek to his chest and cried. In her head, she saw the rest of the scene play out.

The water sucked her under, but somehow she still held onto the gun. For a full minute, she held her breath, not caring what happened to her. But then her body jerked, and her lungs screamed. She wanted to live, to get air. She had to get air. So she kicked her legs and surfaced.

The river had swept her along around a bend and out of sight. She could no longer see the men, nor Andy and his slumped dead figure on the bank. Kicking and sputtering, she was pulled along with the current. It took everything she had to fight back to the bank from which she had come. She didn't want to land on the side with the men.

After what seemed like forever, she caught herself on a half sunk dead log. The roots stuck out under the water, and she braced her feet against them, clinging to the slick surface with all her might. Slowly, she inched her way closer to the shore until she was able to drag her body up onto it.

When she finally reached the muddy mix of dirt and grass on the bank, it felt like the most beautiful hand caressing her face. She pressed her forehead to it a moment, gasping out sobs before realizing she was making too much noise.

Fear snaked through her, even though logically she knew she was so far down river that the men would never catch her. A shot of adrenaline coursed through her blood and she scrambled into the tree line and underneath the nearest bush.

Curling into a wet shaking ball, she cried silently. She didn't come out for two days.

CHAPTER FIFTEEN_
COLE

THAT NIGHT SHE LET HIM CRAWL INTO BED WITH HER. THE narrow mattress gave up a creak as he shifted his hip onto it and watched her make room for him. She was so beautiful, with her sad dark eyes and swollen lips. He wondered if she realized how often she nibbled on them, causing them to redden and puff up.

And how badly did he want to kiss her just now? He was sure she knew how bad. Her hips were pressed into his, her face against his chest, there was no hiding how he felt. But as hard as it was to resist, and it was damn hard, he didn't press his advantage.

Instead, he let his hand stroke down her arm, then travel along the length of her back. With her head nestled into his chest, he could feel her breathing against his bare skin. She shivered once, twice. It didn't make things easier on him. It took every ounce of willpower inside of him to stop there, but he did stop.

She wasn't ready for what came next, not after crying over her dead husband all day. And if he was being honest with himself, he wanted to wait just a bit longer. When he finally got her under him, he wanted to make sure he was the only man on her mind.

Then there were the marks.

What he'd read on her back had him scratching his head. It didn't make a whole lot of sense. Maybe he was interpreting them wrong. It had been dark after all, with his heart hammering a million miles an hour. He'd only glimpsed them for a minute really before lowering her shirt back down.

What he really needed was for Chan to look at them in the daylight. The marks were faded, like a reverse suntan, with the writing being ultra-white and the skin around it being darker.

For days after, he'd wracked his brain, trying to come up with a way to permanently write on someone's skin like that. It wasn't a tattoo, it wasn't ink or raised like a scar. The marks had been smooth, imperceptible to the touch.

Then his mind flicked back to the feel of her skin beneath his fingertips, and he almost groaned out loud. He did want her. Oh, he wanted her bad.

Hannah shifted in his arms then, tilting her face up to look at him. In the cast of moonlight from the window, he could see her eyes staring into his. And then suddenly all of his good intentions seemed to evaporate. Cole's body tensed as his blood pounded through his veins. It had been years since he'd slept with a woman. *Years.*

Raising his hand, he let his fingers trace down the side of her cheek before tucking a loose strand of hair behind her ear. He craved this woman. He wanted her to be his in every way.

What could one little kiss hurt? He thought.

He'd stop after that.

Sliding his fingers down, Cole cupped her chin in his hand and slowly, haltingly, pressed his mouth against hers. The contact lit every nerve in his body on fire. In a breath, he was swamped with it and swamped with her. Then she was kissing him back, parting her lips and he heard himself moan.

It had been so long, so very long since he had done this and since she'd arrived, he'd imagined a thousand ways this would go down. He'd pictured all of the bad things he wanted to do to her, wanted to do to her mouth and to every other part of her body.

He'd sworn he would go slow, he'd sworn he would make her come before him, but now he wasn't sure if he'd make it more than thirty seconds. His hands shot under her shirt, seeking the full breasts that had returned to her body. She moved into his touch, her skin was so soft.

Rolling her onto her back, Cole kept kissing her, still tasting the sweetness of her mouth. They weren't close enough. He had to get closer.

Settling his hips between her legs, he felt a sudden surge as she arched to meet him.

Oh shit, this was going too fast. It was too much, too fast. Breaking the kiss, he pushed back slightly so he could look at her. She blinked up at him, eyes cloudy, lips full. She wanted him right? This wasn't just him.

"You sure about this?" Cole asked, panting. "I can stop. Do you want to stop?"

Hannah nibbled on her lip and reached up, running her hands from his shoulders down his chest, making a skipping trail down to his stomach, then lower. Holy shit, he thought, and it was his last coherent one.

His mouth returned to hers for a moment before drifting down to kiss and lick at her neck. Pulling up on her shirt, he felt her wriggle and arch her back as he worked it over her head. When she brushed her nipples against his chest, he swore under his breath.

Quickly, he ducked his head and sucked first one into his mouth, then the other. She was the one to moan this time but instead of feeling triumph, he only felt more desperate for her. As Hannah cupped his hips, her hands stilled, her fingers pulsing along his sides. He was so hard it fucking hurt now and he groaned softly into the smooth skin of her chest as she rocked back and forth against him.

The way she moved, tilting her hips and letting out those little panting sighs had him on edge, completely at the edge. But there was no stopping now, there just wasn't any stopping.

Lifting his eyes to hers he watched for her reaction as he slipped his hand into her shorts and let his fingers play between her thighs. She was hot, so hot and damp. It rushed through him, heating his blood, though he didn't think any was making it up to his brain at the moment.

Using his thumb he circled against her top before entering her with one finger. She gasped, her eyes growing wide a moment before she closed them. A low moan worked its way from her throat and left him feeling heady.

He stroked her slowly, as slowly as he could manage. Holding one hand between her legs he kept time with the rocking of her hips, careful not to change his pace as she moved quicker beneath him. She was close now, had to be, and he just couldn't wait any longer, he couldn't.

Withdrawing his hand he sat back on his knees and pulled off her shorts completely. She looked... so so good. Twisting and writhing on her back, Hannah's eyes remained closed but her body told him she wanted more. More of him.

Licking at his bottom lip, Cole pushed down on his own boxers then lowered himself between her legs. When he slid inside of her, he covered her mouth with his own, swallowing the gasping little cries she made. She felt... Shit...so good.

As he worked himself in and out of her, he thought he just might explode. In and out. He focused. In and... huffing out a breath, he suddenly couldn't breathe.

Then she was calling out to him, moaning and clenching around him. She was coming. He felt every pulse she made.

Cursing, he quickened his strokes until he too found his release. He stilled a moment, trying to get his breath before collapsing down. His head swam and his heart pounded, he only managed to catch his weight at the last second.

"I'm sorry," he murmured into her hair, inhaling her scent. "You're just so perfect, I couldn't last with you."

"I've never felt like that," she gasped, then placed little kisses all long his cheeks and the scruff of his jaw. "Is it supposed to feel like that?"

At first, he huffed out a laugh, thinking for sure she was teasing him. But then he rolled to the side and pulled her against him. After pressing his lips to her own, he picked his head up and looked down at her.

She blinked at him expectantly.

He frowned.

"What do you mean?"

"Like... that feeling," she said, a blush painting her cheeks. "It aches, but a really good ache and then... you know."

"You *have* had sex before, right?"

"Of course." She nodded seriously, her doe eyes staring into his.

"And what did that feel like to you?" His gut churned a bit, not sure he wanted the answer.

"Well it hurt, you know at first." Hannah scrunched up her face as if she were thinking. "But then it mostly didn't feel like anything at all. Only sometimes it was okay, but not like that."

"Okay..." Cole blew out a breath and rolled onto his back. The Andy guy was dead already so there wasn't any use wanting to kick his ass. "Were you only ever with Andy?"

Hannah went still and silent. Cole could feel her trying

not to squirm next to him. He was such an idiot asking her a question like that. God only knew what terrible things had happened to her out there. Alone. That's why he never pushed her to answer any of the team's questions. The ones about if there were other women, and if so, where.

Rolling back onto his side, Cole propped himself up with one elbow and looked down at her. She was so pretty, truly. In the moonlight her features were soft and her golden hair lay mussed beneath her on the pillow. He wanted to kiss her just then. Again and then again. But there was something else.

He really didn't know that much about her, really hadn't known her for that long. And in that moment, he wanted so desperately to ask her about the marks on her back. But he didn't want to ruin what had just happened between them and clearly she had things she didn't want to say... yet.

So he coached himself to be patient. There would be time.

CHAPTER SIXTEEN_
LIAM

THEY'D DONE IT. COLE FINALLY CLOSED THE DEAL, IT WAS the word on everyone's lips. Their camp was a small one, with Cole's cabin no more than twenty feet from the fire. Sure it had been late, dark out even, with the stars littering the sky. But half the crew had still been up playing cards.

The only place light enough to see the game was around the fire and so they'd heard everything. Well, to be honest, Cookie, Ace and Ryder had heard everything, the fucking perverts. Liam had shoved up to standing and then taken a walk. He just couldn't sit through it.

It wasn't that he was noble or anything, far from it. But the sounds she made, the female moaning… it made him want too much. So he'd gotten up and taken a quick hike down to the creek.

For a while, Liam listened to the water run, letting his eyes play over the far tree line and the fence just beyond it. Then he climbed to the upper border and checked on Chan who was on watch duty. They chit-chatted a bit, talked shop, so to speak. Who got to go on the next raid? Would they be able to swing one before winter? How was progress coming on the new building?

But in the end it was all meaningless talk. It did nothing to save Liam from himself. It did nothing to save him from his own desires.

Hours later, when the fire was good and low and no one was left sitting around it, Liam returned to his own cabin. He pushed open the front door and crouched by his wood burning forge. It was a real one, with a hand crank for air flow and bricks to retain the heat. They'd discovered the thing in the barn of that old farmhouse.

Apparently whomever lived there had dabbled in black smithery because they'd found all the knife making tools Liam could ever need. He'd gotten lucky. Yeah, *that* time, Liam was the lucky one.

He huffed out a breath now and murmured to himself. *Lucky.* The word tasted bitter on his tongue.

Before long the kindling lit and then the small split logs. The thing had no door. The fire just jumped and crackled there in the box, building heat all the while. Standing back, Liam rested his hands on top of his head and arched his back, trying to stretch out the tension. But the tension refused to ease. It wasn't the type to go away quickly.

He was happy for Cole, really he was. They had known each other forever, been the best of friends, closer than brothers even. If any of them deserved to be with a woman again, it was Cole. It certainly wasn't Liam, he would be the first to admit it.

Looking around the sparse room, he sighed. And what would he have for her anyway, if he had been the one? His mattress lay on the floor, he hadn't bothered with a platform, didn't need one. There was no chair inside. If he wanted to sit, then he worked out in his shop. It was just three feet from the front door.

He had no fancy blanket, opting instead to throw his bedroll down on the mattress when he was home. The thing was dirty too, he couldn't recall the last time he'd bothered to wash it. Cole kept up on that kind of stuff. Liam didn't bother.

It hadn't always been that way, though. There was a time before the war when they had shared an apartment in college. Liam had more crisp clothes in his closet than Cole ever thought about having. He kept everything looking sharp too, and the girls down there were... well, plentiful.

It had been humid, Liam recalled, even sticky at times. Tulane was right on the gulf, with the Mississippi River on the other side. Baton Rouge wasn't so far off and the night scene in Louisiana was something else entirely. How did they end up there?

Liam shook his head at the memory. They were just two boys from Pennsylvania just looking for something else, somewhere else. Baseball had gotten them both accepted though. Scholarships. God, how things were different back then.

When was the last time he'd played a game? Liam

rubbed a hand down his face and sighed. He'd never pick up a ball again.

An hour later, Liam lay awake on his mattress, staring up at the ceiling. Sleep just wouldn't come, and thoughts of her... they kept washing over him. The way her golden hair shined in the sun, the flash in her eyes as she pressed the hilt of the knife to his back. Cole's little shadow... Cole's.

Tossing aside his sleeping bag, Liam scrambled up and shoved out the door. The night air was cold, winter was a heartbeat away and they weren't nearly as prepared as they ought to be.

In his shop, there was an old lantern. He fetched a small stick and went back to his cabin, holding the end in the fire. Upon returning, he lifted the glass carefully and lit the wick that stuck up from the oil. This was a precious resource and he rarely ever used it, but tonight, he needed it.

Rummaging around in his box of raw material, Liam nearly emptied the damn thing searching for just the right stuff.

He knew it was crazy. He knew he would never, ever be able to give it to her. But something inside of him urged Liam to make it anyway.

Finding the small pieces he was looking for, he collected them all up and put them into one of his metal casting molds. These particular tools were a necessary part of his trade. Blowing out the lamp, Liam returned to his cabin and set the mold inside of his forge using a pair of tongs. After that he began shoving piece after piece of wood in the fire. It would need to get really hot before everything melted down.

Crossing to the front door, Liam propped it open, then moved over to the solitary window and lifted it up, too. It was going to feel like a million degrees in here but he had all night long. And that was alright with him, really it was. This was the closest to okay he'd felt since Cole had ridden up their road with Hannah clutched in his arms.

CHAPTER SEVENTEEN_
HANNAH

IT WAS THE SAME DREAM EVERY TIME SHE HAD IT. THE WILD grass on the ground was wet with dew. It was early morning. The air had a chill, a dampness to it, but it wasn't icy cold. She blinked into awareness. She heard a sound like a dull ringing in her ears.

The first thing she could feel was pain, a stabbing aching sort of pain in her right hand, so she looked down. She was bleeding.

Big streaks of bright red blood were pouring from the back of her hand. There was a hole in it, sort of. It didn't go all the way through, but it was deep, right between her thumb and first finger. She sucked in a breath and then he was yelling at her.

She looked up, because he had risen to standing and she was still kneeling in the grass.

Run! Come on, Hannah run! We've got to go now!

It was Andy, with his blue eyes wide with panic and his

strawberry blonde hair hidden beneath a black ball cap. He reached for their backpacks and grabbed her hand, the one with the wound. The pain of his grasp sent spikes shooting down her arm but it got her attention and she began to move.

Don't look back! Don't look, just keep going!

They were entering the trees then, jumping roots and dodging bushes. And the vacancy in her mind, that big white blank page, it felt more immense than it ever had. She could hear his harsh breathing that mirrored her own, could feel the way the adrenaline pumped through her body, making her seem as if she could fly.

But then she did it. She disobeyed him. But he never found out about it.

Hannah looked over her shoulder. She looked back at what they were running from. The sight of it would never... ever leave her.

Waking with a gasp, Hannah sat up in bed, still panting. Her body was jolting. She needed to run. Run for her life. It was sunrise in Cole's cabin. The grayness of the morning was seeping in through the window above his bed.

Running shaky fingers through her hair, she exhaled slowly, then looked at the scar still visible on her right hand. That's where he had cut her. Andy always denied it, and she had no absolute memory of it, but somethings you just *know*.

"Hey," Cole murmured sleepily and reached for her. "You okay?"

"Yeah, just a bad dream."

"Will you share it with me?"

Cole rolled up onto his side and ran his hand along her arm. His eyes had cleared and he looked thoughtful, but he waited with his usual level of patience. Hannah glanced away, out the window. There was a mist drifting through the trees, giving them an otherworldly appearance. It was beautiful. She sighed.

"That's alright," Cole said finally.

Wrapping his hand gently around the back of her neck he dragged her down to him, down to press her mouth against his, to kiss her. Immediately she softened, feeling the new heat that his touch brought to her skin.

Snuggling in close to him, she explored his body with her hands while his kisses traveled to her neck, then to her shoulders. When he stopped, she let a slow smile fill her face. He was watching her, those green eyes so deep and intense. Reaching up, he ran his thumb gently over her lips. She liked everything he did to her. He made her never want to leave his bed.

"I want you to trust me," he said, his face suddenly serious. "No matter what, I will always protect you. I want you to stay with me. Will you?"

She nodded at him then, feeling with every ounce of her body that she would stay. And then he was on her, and in her, and she felt swept away just like the night before.

The things he did to her, the way he made her body

build and clench and release. It was unlike anything she'd ever known. *He* was unlike anyone she had ever known, and she only ever wanted more.

After it was over, he lay on his back and pulled her on top of him. Stroking at her hair, he placed deliberate kisses on her forehead and she fell back asleep.

An hour later when she woke, she was all alone. He had stoked the fire in the cabin so it was warm, and for a minute she just lay there naked in his bed. It was cold outside, and getting colder with each day.

Sitting up, she placed a palm against the glass of the window pane above his bed and felt the chill. Cole had told her that she could wear anything that belonged to him, so she crossed to his dresser and picked through his clothes. They were all so much bigger than her that it was laughable.

Selecting a long sleeve maroon shirt, she slipped it over her head and felt the material stop just a few inches below her butt. It was practically a dress. Then she found a pair of boxer briefs but they didn't want to stay up around her waist. Only the one pair seemed small enough to cling to her and those needed a good wash.

Absently, she wondered how she would go about doing that here. She made a note to ask Cole and continued picking through his things. Though none of his pants fit her, she did find an oversized sweatshirt and shrugged into it. It was dark gray and a little dusty and could probably use a wash, too.

Finally slipping into a pair of his socks, Hannah

grabbed her new brush off the dresser. She ran it through her hair, smoothing out the tangles until it felt neat enough and then opened the door to go outside.

The sun was rising higher in the sky but it hadn't been up long enough to chase the cold from the air. Goosebumps stood out on her exposed legs but there wasn't really anything she could do about it, and the three months she spent without pants had gotten her used to the feeling. Of course that had been in the height of summer, thankfully.

Most of the men were ranged around the fire. The smell of breakfast permeated the air. Cookie was poking and prodding the food, grumbling like he always was while Davey and Ace laughed at something.

Standing further behind them, at the far edge of the split log benches, Cole and Chan had their heads close together, locked in quiet discussion. At the sight of her, all activity stopped.

She could feel their eyes upon her and as usual it was an uncomfortable feeling. A feeling she had been schooled by Andy to avoid at all costs. Glancing down, she felt her cheeks blush and worked to remind herself that she was safe here. Her fingers twisted and twined themselves together in front of her but the smell of food had her stomach grumbling.

Despite her nerves, she kept walking forward until her eyes found a log bench and she sat, keeping her gaze averted. The silence was deafening.

"Good morning, Little Miss." Cookie cleared his throat

and she could hear him continue to stir whatever was in the pot.

"Good morning," Hannah responded, and lifted her head.

They were all grinning at her. Davey and Ace, Ryder and Cookie. She heard them each offer her a *good morning* and it had her smiling back at them, but she didn't know why.

"What?" She asked.

"Hey, we got you a present," Davey spoke up. Quiet, reserved Davey. The one who had barely said a word to her in a month.

"Oh?"

"Cole mentioned you needed some shoes," he explained.

Reaching behind him Davey grabbed a pair of small black boots and stood up. He crossed to her and held them out, a look of pride filling his features. Hannah stood up too and accepted his gift. Turning them over in her hands she gasped. Cole had said Davey was handy, always figuring out a way to build something from nothing, but this was beyond her comprehension.

"They're amazing," Hannah beamed, turning a full smile on him that made Davey's cheeks pink. "How did you do it?"

"I found a pair no one was using and took them all apart, then had to cut everything smaller and re-stitch it all back together. I'm only sorry it took so long. I hope they fit."

"Wow, just..." Hannah paused, trying to find the right words as tears filled her eyes.

She couldn't say what it was like to walk this country in bare feet, feeling every rock and stick and thorn. For months and months, not thinking you'd make it when the snow hit the ground, wondering if you'd eventually lose feeling in them.

"Hey, try them on." Davey reached out and gave her shoulder a little shake, then let his hand slide down her arm.

"Thank you," she whispered. "Thank you so, so much."

Dropping to the bench, she dusted off the bottoms of her socks and loosened the laces on the boots. She slipped one foot inside and then hurried to put the other one on. They were still a hair big, but it was better than having them too small. Another pair of socks would make the fit just right. She laced them up snugly and then stood up and stomped around. She heard a round of applause and some laughter.

"They're perfect," she announced.

Throwing a look over her shoulder at all the guys, Hannah noted their happy faces. But standing further back, Cole wasn't smiling. He didn't look unhappy exactly, but his expression was one of concern. Only when he caught her gaze did he force a broad smile and give her a thumbs up. Chan nodded, too.

Something was off with him, but she knew better than to let the knowledge show on her face. Keeping up appearances she let herself get sucked into conversation with

Davey, who sat beside her for the first time. It was thrilling to have the boots and she let herself enjoy the feeling, even though it was dampened a bit by the edge on Cole. Later. She would find out later what was the matter.

Breakfast itself was good, something Cookie called cornbread pancakes. Hannah watched him carefully, thinking it would probably be wise to learn how he did it. He had a batter of sorts that he stirred in the pot and then scooped a few spoonfuls onto a smooth black griddle to heat. Once they were bubbling, he used a metal spatula to flip them over and finish cooking the other side.

"Can I help you?" Hannah asked, approaching him near the end of the meal.

"With what?"

"Anything."

Cookie eyed her speculatively between bites of the yellow crumbly cake. Finally he huffed a breath and nodded once. "You could grind the corn into powder for me. The dried stalks are down in the cellar but I could pull them up for you and show you how to do it."

"Alright." Hannah's heart beat a little faster. She'd do almost anything to get inside that storage building.

Cookie's eyes flitted behind her and she followed his gaze to where Cole was watching them. He couldn't quite hide his frown, so instead he turned away.

"You can come by tomorrow," Cookie said, drawing her attention back to him. "And don't mind Cole. If you're going to stay, then you'll have to get to know everyone. He can't have you all to himself."

Hannah nodded, still feeling a bit uncertain until Cookie gave her a wink. He was right, surely, and she *did* want to stay. Wanted it more than anything. This place already felt more like home to her than anywhere she could remember being. Even in her memory of the doctor, the room they had been in had felt... restricting.

But here at the compound, they ate well, slept on beds, there was no violence or fear. She wanted it to stay exactly the way it was. She wanted to contribute even, to pull her own weight, to help.

"Can I wash the dishes?" Hannah ventured, and was rewarded with Cookie's burst of laughter.

He gestured to a pot of fresh water that he had warming over the fire before nodding towards a bar of soap sitting on a low wood table just a few feet away. The table was always positioned there and it belonged exclusively to Cookie. He had his things strewn across it, including a sort of raised wooden rack for drying dishes.

Crossing to the pot Hannah worked deliberately, enjoying the way the warm water felt on her hands and arms as she scrubbed at the dishes with the bar of soap. When she was done with one, she walked it over to the table and propped it up in the rack.

Davey lingered close by, talking about the process of making the soap from ash and animal fat. She bobbed her head every once in a while and glanced up at him. He would grin sheepishly, but it didn't stop him from talking.

It felt good. He was nice. She was making friends, she

thought. Yes, *friends* was the right word. Her temple gave a slight throb before quieting.

"When they're all done you can stack them back in storage." Cookie handed her an empty pot. "You'll see the shelf for them right when you walk in the door."

Nodding, Hannah's hands began to shake. Quickly, she dunked them back in the water so no one would notice. She would get to go inside the long building. She would get to see more of the things in there. More cans. Maybe more memories.

The anticipation of remembering something new made her insides quiver. She hurried to wash the rest.

CHAPTER EIGHTEEN_
COLE

HE DIDN'T WANT TO LEAVE HER THERE. HE DIDN'T WANT TO let her out of his sight. Since that moment on the road when he watched her hold a gun to her own head, he knew he had to keep her alive at all costs. But now Cole was forced to admit, it wasn't just that anymore. He wanted her with him constantly. To make certain no one could touch her, or hurt her, or have her.

But Trey had come to him after breakfast with a question about the new build. It was something Cole needed to see for himself and unfortunately it just couldn't wait. The construction had been delayed long enough already. With Hannah's arrival and everyone kind of scrambling around, they were behind schedule, big time.

So Cole had left Hannah behind to wash dishes and followed Trey to the clearing near the top of the property. The spot had a great view on all sides but was still easily defended, tucked up underneath a few remaining trees.

Once completed, the new building would become their central gathering place. It would be far larger than anything they had constructed so far and most of it would be made with stone. Stone doesn't burn. You learn that the hard way when you watch everything else catch on fire.

"So I'm having a hell of a time bracing this wall," Trey was talking.

As he explained the problem, he gestured to the internal dividing wall they wanted on the inside of the structure. The building would be split in half, with a main room that had a fireplace, tables and chairs, maybe even a few benches or a couch if they could swing it. The other room would be a bunk house. In the dead of winter, or under siege, they would all be able to hole up in there.

Cole listened to Trey's issues and made some mental notes of his own. He would need to assign more guys to this project. He would need to give up some of his time with Hannah and contribute as well. To say he had been distracted over the past month was an understatement. He hadn't even realized how much until presented with the lack of progress before him.

"Do you know how much wood we've split so far?" Cole interrupted.

"Not enough," Trey admitted.

"I was really hoping to have this thing done before winter," Cole said, almost to himself. "But in order to do so, I'll have to pull guys off wood cutting and it seems we're behind on that, too."

"Yeah," Trey agreed, but didn't offer any solutions. That wasn't his deal.

It was Cole's job to come up with the solutions, and usually he did. But how was he going to swing this one? Cole climbed into the structure. Crouching down, he poked at this and then stood and pushed his toe against that. All the while, his mind was running through scenarios.

"It looks good so far, Trey," Cole said finally, stepping back. "I'm going to go ask around and send up the help you need today. Alright?"

"Sounds good boss, thanks."

Cole nodded his head and turned to go. He hiked back down the hillside and headed for the fire ring where he had last seen Hannah. She'd looked happy, relaxed even, and the boots from Davey were just right. It wasn't that he didn't want those things for her, he did. He wanted the guys to accept her and for her to fit in and live here.

But at the same time, watching the way Davey got close to her, touched her even, it made something inside Cole coil up. He had to work in order to ease it back down.

And now they all knew he'd slept with her, like *actually* slept with her. The moment he'd walked outside this morning, the cat calls had started. At first, Cole had smiled at their teasing and maybe even joked along.

But then something about it changed. There was an undercurrent of testing there, like they wanted to know just how far they could push him. And of course none of them said it outright, but he knew what they were thinking. They wanted to know if they would get a chance with her, and if so, when. Last girl on earth and all that.

It pissed Cole off and if he was being honest, it scared him just a little. None of them were violent with women, they'd all been together long enough for him to know that. But a man was only a man after all, and he wondered how long they would stay here when they realized it would only be to look at Hannah, nothing more.

These were his friends, his brothers, the only family he had left. The thought of even one of them leaving made him sick. Looking down now, Cole could see the fire ring and the collection of cabins just beyond. Eyes scanning, he didn't see Hannah anywhere.

His stomach dropped a bit and he hurried his pace, picking up to a jog as he slid down the slope. All of the guys were standing at the threshold to the storage building, looking inside. He counted them. One, two, three, four as his breath started hitching. No Hannah. Where the fuck was Hannah.

Skidding to a stop behind the group, he yanked back on Cookie's shoulder so that he faced him.

"Where is she?" Cole's voice came out breathless.

"Inside." Cookie gestured to the doorway. "She's just been touching things and asking about them."

"Touching things?" Cole's eyebrows raised in question.

"Everything." Cookie shrugged. "Like she's never seen any of it before."

Cole squeezed past the others who barely gave him a passing glance and entered the dimly lit storage building. It had a few windows but they weren't the kind that opened. They were wide and short, placed at the very top of the walls, positioned in such a way that they let just enough light in to see by.

His heart was still thundering in his chest, but then there she was, just as Cookie had described. She had taken off his sweatshirt and rolled up the sleeves of his shirt, leaving her hair to flow down her back. It had grown warmer. The sun was up and it would prove to be one of the last nice days of the year.

At first, she didn't notice him come in. Instead, she faced the wall of shelves with all of the goods their team had accumulated over the years. Cole approached her, licking his lips, trying to calm the fear that had spiked so unnecessarily in his blood stream. She was safe here with them, he had to remember that.

"Hannah?" He kept his voice quiet, she seemed so focused just then. "What are you doing?"

She turned to look at him over her shoulder. Those big dark eyes were focused far off someplace else. It was a look she wore often.

"Hmm?" She hummed it, then looked down at the object she was clutching in her hands. "Coca Cola," she said, then after a pause she added, "you drink it."

"Yeah." Cole frowned. "Do you want some?"

Hannah looked back down at the soda, then closed her eyes and pressed it to her forehead. After inhaling a long breath, she opened her eyes and replaced it on the shelf.

"No," she said.

For several minutes, Cole watched her select items from the shelves and examine them. She would hold them tightly in her hands, and if they didn't have a label, she would turn to the doorway and hold whatever it was up.

The guys would call out then, telling her the name and what it was used for. She would reward them with a dazzling smile and repeat it back to them. It had them chuckling, like a game, but it was freaking Cole out. Freaking him out bad.

He thought back to the marks, the ones he had read again just that morning. After she fell back asleep, he had scooted out from under her and ran his hands along her spine. The code was the same as he saw before and again it left him puzzled. That was the reason he had left her alone in the cabin and come outside in the first place... to find Chan.

And after the teasing and other shit had died down, he'd tracked Chan down, pulling him aside and whispering in his ear. Then Cole had drawn the marks in the dirt as accurately as he could.

Chan just shook his head slowly and couldn't figure it out either. He wanted to see it on her, of course. Cole would be forced to confront Hannah about it soon but now obviously wasn't a good time.

"Hey, Han." Cole stepped closer, intercepting her before she could select another can or box or bag. "I could really use your help."

The genuine smile that had lit up Hannah's face faded,

and for a moment, Cole regretted his words. But then she recovered in an instant and bobbed her head in acceptance.

"Sure." She grabbed onto his elbow. "What do you need?"

He led her outside while the other guys grumbled good-naturedly about Cole ending all the fun. Turning to each of them, he handed out the new assignments and as briefly as possible explained himself.

Cookie would take first watch duty and have to stay through a second as well. Ryder, Davey and Chan needed to report to the new build site to help Trey. Ace would continue to cut wood, then switch out with Cookie for the third watch rotation.

They would keep that schedule until the stone building was complete. Cole would step in to supplement Cookie's wood cutting shift (the older man made meals and so didn't typically have any obligations other than watch) and Liam would go up to the build site.

As the men dispersed, Cole glanced around. Where was Liam anyway?

"So what can I do?" Hannah asked, interrupting his thoughts.

"Well..." Cole scrambled to come up with something... anything. "You could collect kindling and small branches. Have you ever made tinder bundles?"

"Sure." Hannah brightened at the suggestion and it had the tightness in Cole's chest easing.

After he found Liam and explained the new assignment, he would go up to start cutting wood with Ace. If Hannah was collecting small branches and stuff then she would be close to him. He could keep an eye on her. It was the perfect plan.

Glancing up to the hillside, Cole eyed Liam's cabin. The door to his shop was closed which meant he wasn't working up there. When Liam wasn't making knives, the next best place to look for him was always with the animals. He was probably in the pasture, checking sheep or fence. It was possible he was on the far side, looking over the hay stack and the tarps they had acquired.

Taking Hannah by the hand, Cole let his lips brush against her cheek as they began to walk. It felt so good to have her next to him. The feel of her hand in his was just right. Briefly, his worry returned about her odd behavior in storage, but then they were at the pasture gate and pushing through it.

Cole's eyes scanned for Liam and spied him crouched down at the edge of the creek, a large mound of dirt was piled next to him on the bank. What was he doing?

As they got closer, what Cole thought was a mound of dirt was actually a pile of clothing heaped beneath Liam's sleeping bag. The man was washing everything, actually honestly washing everything.

Cole's mouth dropped in surprise a moment before they stopped beside Liam. Letting go of Hannah's hand, Cole crouched down, a slight grin tweaking his features.

"What are you doing?" He asked.

"What's it look like?" Liam muttered.

Glancing up, he looked past Cole and zeroed in on

Hannah. Liam nodded his head at her once before grabbing for another shirt and dunking it in the stream of water. She's finally getting to him, Cole realized. It was the first time his friend hadn't frowned or sneered or made some damning comment before shunning her.

Maybe if he could get Liam on his side, then the others would figure it out, too. There had to be a way they could all stay here; had to be a way they could keep their team together and add Hannah to it.

"Looks like you're using soap. Didn't know you had it in you," Cole commented.

"There was a time-" Liam looked up at him, hands covered in suds as he rubbed the bar against the soaking material. "That I could clean you under the table, my friend."

"Tulane?" Cole snorted at the memory.

College, apartment, girls. Liam had really come into his own then. No more foster care. No more black eyes and strange bruises. Though his last home *had* been a decent one, and more often than not, he'd slept at Cole's house.

"You were the hot mess back then." Liam squinted up at Hannah again, watching her. "Guess I just forgot who I was for a while."

"Indeed." Cole nodded sagely. "Well, as much as I support this new habit, you're going to have to save it for another day."

"There won't be many good days after this one," Liam protested, continuing to wash. "I'll need the sun to dry everything out."

"Well, we're behind on the stone house and wood cutting, too. It's all hands on deck."

"Even your hands?"

"Yes asshole, even mine."

"Well, I'm halfway through." Liam stood and carried the clean wet shirt to a nearby bush and spread it out to dry. "I can't just leave it all now."

"I'll do it," Hannah's voice piped up, causing both men to look at her. "I'll finish washing your things."

"What?" Cole asked. If she finished Liam's laundry, then he'd have to leave her down here all by herself. The thought unnerved him.

"You'd wash my stuff?" Liam was staring at her, one hand raised, shading his eyes.

"Sure." Hannah's voice was quiet, but she didn't look away from him. "Why wouldn't I?"

"Well-" Liam looked around him then, his arms gesturing to the pile on the ground. "It's all dirty."

"I've been dirty, Liam," Hannah reminded him. "I may not be able to make knives like you or chop wood, but I'm not useless."

"That's not what I meant," Liam mumbled the words and Cole watched his friend look properly lost for the briefest moment.

"I want to help," Hannah went on, her voice gaining in strength as she went. "I can work, let me work."

"Alright." Liam looked from her to Cole, then back again. "Okay."

Hannah beamed in triumph and Cole couldn't help but

smile at her small victory. She wanted to prove herself, she wanted to contribute. That meant she wanted to stay. And to have Liam, who so obviously and adamantly disapproved of her from the start, accept her... well that was a really good sign.

She brushed past Cole as he rose to standing and patted at his cheek briefly before stooping to collect the sleeping bag. Suddenly, Cole remembered that meant he had to leave her alone, and it was something he absolutely did not want to do.

As Liam grabbed for his socks and boots, Cole scrambled for an excuse not to agree to this arrangement. But it was too late. There was no way he could risk crushing what Hannah had just accomplished. Liam had accepted her help, she was working to benefit the group as a whole, that was it.

So, even though every part of Cole screamed at him not to walk away from her, he did. Though every part of him wanted to run back and drag her along beside him, he resisted. Side by side with Liam, he trudged up to the top of the pasture and through the fence. But that didn't mean he didn't look back.

They both did.

CHAPTER NINETEEN_
LIAM

THAT NIGHT, WHEN LIAM GOT BACK TO HIS CABIN ALL OF HIS things were neatly folded and waiting for him on his mattress. He was tired and his back ached from working at the build site all day, but the second he saw his clothes sitting there, all that other stuff just floated away. She had been here, without him, inside his home.

Glancing around the small space he suddenly wished for a broom, or a dust thingy. It looked shabby and run down to him. He hadn't wanted her to see it like that. But with a shake of his head, he reminded himself that Hannah would not be staying with him, not ever. So it didn't matter.

When he had first come in, he lit the fire so the light was picking up a bit now. Crossing to his bed, Liam knelt down on the floor and ran one hand over the clean sleeping bag. It was dry and crisp, the way everything was when you set it out all day in the sun. He hadn't told her thank you, he realized, and his brow furrowed at the slip. He would remember next time he saw her.

Carefully, he picked up each tidy pile she had made and set them next to his bed on the floor. There was a stack of shirts, a stack of pants, even his socks were matched and folded together.

He couldn't help but smile to himself at that. He didn't think anyone in his whole life had ever done his laundry for him. Well maybe his mom had back when he was a real little kid, he corrected, but it wasn't something he could recall. The feeling it left him with was... new.

Spreading out his sleeping bag, Liam stripped out of his dirty clothes and into a fresh pair of underwear. His hands were filthy. The dirt traveled all the way up his arms, ran along the back of his neck and around to his face. He should keep a bucket of clean water in here, he thought before stepping to add a log to the fire. Then he could wash himself before bed and keep his sleeping bag nicer.

Stepping back, he watched the flames dance inside his forge for a few moments more. As he lay down for the night, he let his thoughts travel back to the build site and the work they had accomplished that day. Cole had been right to switch out the assignments. It was definitely needed, and they had made good progress already.

Working with Trey and Ryder though, had proved to be a bit of a challenge. More so than in the past. Liam's former scowl returned to his face. Davey was alright and Chan of course kept quiet, but the others, they just wouldn't shut up.

"Man, I could listen to her all night long," Ryder had said while he hauled stones from the far pile to the wall.

"Bullshit, you couldn't make her sound like that all night long," Trey countered, and had everyone chuckling. Even Liam had smirked at that point.

"But seriously-" Ryder hefted another rock. "How's this going to work? Like do we go in a certain order, or maybe draw straws, or what?"

"Oh, you think you're going to get a turn?" Davey asked.

"Why not?"

"Well, she's not a damn carousel ride at the fair, ya fuckin' neanderthal," Davey quipped and had everyone hooting.

Everyone but Liam.

Ryder was Davey's younger brother, like by blood, so Davey knew just what to say to skirt an actual fight. Which was good, it kept Liam from starting one.

"He should let her hang out more, though," Trey added after a minute of silence.

"That's all I was saying," Ryder explained. "Like give the rest of us a chance. If she wants to stay here, then we should all get to know her. You know?"

"I don't know man," Trey again. "Eight guys is a lot of dudes, I wouldn't wish that on any girl."

"I've seen it," Ryder said.

"Oh really?" Trey smirked. "Where? Wait... let me guess... the internet."

Everyone busted up laughing again.

Poor Ryder, all the shit he ever talked about had

happened on the internet. Now there was no more internet and there never would be again. At least not in their lifetime. Tech was dead, electricity was dead, the whole wide fucking world was dead. Liam hadn't heard a plane fly overhead in three years, not since their last mission. The sky was silent.

If there was life anywhere else on the planet, then they were in the same piss poor shape that this country was in. Liam shook his head but kept working.

"What if there are more girls out there?" Ryder threw out the idea that was on everyone's mind.

"There aren't any more," Davey reminded him. "We looked."

"Well, we didn't find Hannah," Ryder pointed out. "Maybe we weren't looking in the right spot. Maybe we didn't go far enough."

"You talking about leaving?" Trey asked.

"I'm just saying that it's possible," Ryder answered, and let the conversation die.

Liam's stomach sank then. Damn it, that kind of talk was exactly what he had predicted would happen. Hannah stirred things in all of them that were better left buried. She made each of them want things. Things from before. And in time, Ryder would convince Davey to leave. Trey would probably go with them, figuring the three of them had a better chance together, and they would be right.

That would leave the compound down to five guys. It would be a lot of strain on everyone to keep it going then.

It would be hard to defend and their drop in numbers would eventually become known.

Then the attacks would start again, and this time they might be on the losing side. The same side as those poor bastards in the farmhouse. The ones who had fought like hell only to die gasping for air in the dark, suffocating together over a bunch of stuff. That was the thing about underground bunkers, you cut off the fresh air supply and it's only a matter of time.

CHAPTER TWENTY_
HANNAH

SHE WAS IN THE STOREROOM AGAIN TODAY. ALL AROUND her, the cans, the boxes and bags with their worn labels and dented lids, sat still on the shelves. But none of them opened her mind the way she had hoped, not like that first night with the can of corn. Even though she'd been living at the compound for a few months now, she still couldn't remember anything. It was disappointing to say the least.

Cookie was down in the cellar now. She could hear him talking to himself. He chatted and complained in turn but Hannah thoroughly enjoyed it.

Perched on a small stool, her jacket cinched around her, Hannah stripped dried corn off the stalks and funneled the kernels into her mortar. When she judged she had enough, she set the now empty stalks in a nearby basket.

Later, she would grind those nearly inedible remains down further and feed it to the livestock. The goat in particular enjoyed the crunchy leftovers. But now, with the good kernels in front of her, she worked with her pestle and ground the corn into powder that the entire crew could eat.

Over the sound of her methodic grinding, Hannah could hear the rain begin again. The storeroom had a tin roof, more salvage material that had been taken from somewhere Cole referred to as "the farmhouse." He didn't like to talk about it. In fact, each time it was brought up, his jaw clenched. She couldn't help but wonder about it as he worked his teeth slowly against one another, but then he always managed to change the subject.

"How much have you got?" Cookie stomped up out of the cellar and came to look over her shoulder.

Hannah smiled at the way he clucked his teeth, hovering over her, pretending like she wasn't doing it right. There was something endearing about him because underneath his quirks, she knew he had a heart of gold.

Refusing to stop in her grinding, Hannah simply nodded her head towards the opaque white tub where her final product lay. There weren't very many like it, made of plastic with a lid that sealed on the top. In fact, there were only four, but they contained the most precious of resources.

One for the corn flour, one for dried beans, one for white rice, and one for salt. The rice and salt were dwindling though, and they were something that Cookie confessed could not be resupplied.

"Rain's come again," Cookie observed after failing to find fault with her progress.

"It's a good thing the guys got the roof up over the stone house," Hannah commented. They had worked night and day to get the walls finished and the roof on before the weather turned. Now they all just worked inside of it.

"Yes it is," Cookie agreed, before taking a seat across from her and starting to strip stalks of his own. "It's ready for me to start cooking in and I'll be happy to be out of the wind and the rain."

"Me too." Hannah huffed a breath, pausing a moment to push her hair back over her shoulder.

For an hour or more they actually worked in silence. At first, Hannah hardly noticed it, she was so focused on the task at hand. But then she finished with her grinding and cleaned up her tools and Cookie still had no comment for her.

Unusual. She kept waiting for him to remind her where to store everything, or to question how tightly she sealed the lid, but he didn't. Something was up with him.

"Cookie, is everything alright?"

He glanced up at her, then back down, still intent on his work. His hands were steady but he shifted in his seat. Leaning this way and that, he couldn't quite settle himself properly.

Hannah turned away from him and collected her latest sewing project from the little shelf he had allowed her. She was working on another pair of jeans.

Taking out the knife Liam had given her, Hannah worked to carefully cut the stitches from the man sized pair of pants. She didn't want to cut any of the fabric unnecessarily. Once they were all apart, she would trim them down to her size and hand stitch them back together. You had to be pretty deliberate about the whole thing if you wanted to keep the zipper and button centered.

As she worked across from him, she listened to Cookie begin to grunt, then huff and sigh. It was coming, she knew. Whatever was on his mind was fighting to get out of his mouth. But he didn't want it to, that was the thing. He was actually trying really hard not to say anything, and that in itself made Hannah nervous. She had never known him to hold back.

"There's been talk," Cookie admitted finally.

"What kind of talk?"

"The leaving kind." He winced at the admission, but wouldn't look her in the eye.

"What do you mean leaving? Who's leaving? Why?"

"Some of the young kids," Cookie explained. Hannah knew he meant the rest of the guys. They would always be children in his eyes. "They can't last here anymore. They're talking about moving on."

"But why?"

"Oh, Little Miss." Cookie clucked now, sitting back to look at her sadly. "You really don't know a thing about men, do you?"

Hannah's hands stilled in her cutting and her mouth dropped just a bit. He must be correct in what he said because the implications were beyond her. Again, she felt vulnerable and stupid, thinking that if she could just have her entire memory back, maybe she wouldn't be at such a loss.

Everyone here was working with a full deck of cards, not realizing she was only holding one hand. And she couldn't let them know that. She couldn't.

Every time someone asked her about her home, or where she came from or her last name, she refused to answer. She avoided the questions or found an excuse to slip away. It wasn't because she didn't want to tell them, it was because she didn't know.

"Before you came around, there was no hope," Cookie began. "We spent two years killing in the war, then six months fighting our way up here and then three more months murdering any man within a ten mile radius in order to keep it.

Never once did we see a live woman, not since the tail end of the war. Seen plenty dead though. And it isn't like we didn't search, because we did. But searching is its own dangerous game. It leaves you exposed to being hunted yourself."

"You... murdered people?" Hannah's voice hitched, though she wished it wouldn't.

"Yes dear, we all have. More times over than any of us could count. That's just a stone cold fact."

"Why?"

"For everything you see around you." Cookie gestured to the room at large, but his implication fell over the entire compound. "For shelter and safety. For life and peace. Fact is the others only stopped coming once Liam started gutting em' and hanging em' upside down from the trees at the bottom of the mountain."

Hannah sucked in a breath at that, her stomach flipping inside her. She knew the crew gave Liam a wide berth, but she thought it was because he could be so short. Now she thought maybe it was a touch of fear, too. Fear at what he was capable of.

"So like I said, there was no hope. No women, only us, and that was okay. We were all equal in our hell. All equal in the demons we had become." Cookie paused, thinking a moment before continuing on. "But then there you were. A woman, and a pretty one at that. You've reminded us what it is to be men. Not monsters, but human men."

Cookie looked pointedly at her but Hannah just blinked back at him.

"Now they have hope, right? So why leave?" She asked, finally.

"Because they remember what it's like to hold a woman, to have one, to sleep with one. It makes them want that for themselves."

"Oh." Hannah's heart skipped quickly. "I see."

"Cole is losing his position as leader," Cookie explained. "He has you all to himself, he's made it clear he's not willing to share you. The others have decided there might be more women somewhere else and they want to go find them. They won't stay here and watch the thing they want the rest of their lives without any chance of getting it."

Hannah pushed back abruptly, letting her stool scrape along the wooden floor. The sound was dimmed only by the pounding of the rain on the roof. The storm outside was growing.

Turning away from Cookie, she paced to the wall and tilted her head up to look out one of the high windows. Big round drops splattered against the glass and ran in streaks out of sight.

"You won't answer any questions." Cookie kept his voice soft now. "About where you came from, or if there are more of you. It would help us to know the truth."

Squeezing her eyes shut, Hannah fought the flood of guilt. God she wished more than anything that she had those answers for them. Where had she come from? Were there more like her?

But the truth was, she didn't know. All she had captured in her mind was her time with Andy and that had been brief, without even a hint of other women. But there was that one time, in the months after he'd died. When she'd been wandering around all alone, there was that one place. The bad place.

Sucking in a breath Hannah came to a decision. She couldn't let Cole lose his position because of her. She would tell them all the truth about what she'd seen... even if it meant confessing what a coward she was.

Turning back to face Cookie, she wiped a tear from her eye and resumed her seat. Her chest grew tight with the memory.

"It was dark, I had been wandering alone for a long time," Hannah began. "The forest was thick, so I picked my way slowly because that was the way Andy had taught me.

The loneliness was... overwhelming for me. Andy was dead and I hadn't heard the sound of another person in a month, maybe two."

Hannah let her eyes bounce up to Cookie but he didn't comment, so she went on.

"I should never have gone so close, I should never..." Hannah's breath hitched once more, then evened out. "But I heard crying. Not a rabbit or, or a wounded bird, but a person. A... a woman. The sound was intoxicating almost, it called to me and I had to answer.

I crawled up the side of the nearest hill and I looked down into a tiny gulley. There was a building, not as big as this one, not even as big as Cole's cabin. It was small and thin and tall, made of concrete with a wooden door."

"Go on," Cookie commanded, eager now, leaning forward.

"And then I saw a cage. It had metal bars all around and laying at the bottom was the woman, or what I thought was a woman. Whoever it was, they were crying, it was pitiful. I wasn't thinking clearly. I got up and I started to run. I ran down to the clearing, out of the trees and that's when I saw the man. He was stumbling. I don't know what was wrong with him."

"Was there just the one man?"

"No." Hannah shook her head. "There were more, at least two. I stopped right there and fell flat on my face. I was on my belly in the dirt just yards from their fire, but it was smoldering, almost out and it didn't throw hardly any light.

They could've seen me with the moon, but they were all looking at her and the man was screaming for her to shut up. I was stuck there, it felt like forever, but it couldn't have been more than a few seconds. He banged on the metal cage with his hands and she made this sound, like she was so scared."

Hannah put her hand up to her mouth, remembering the whimper. It had struck such fear inside of her. She had felt the woman's terror in her own body.

"It's okay, Little Miss." Cookie tried to soothe her. "It's alright."

"No." Hannah shook her head. "I just left her there. I got up and I ran. I ran and ran until I couldn't breathe and my feet were bloody and I hid inside a dead log. I'm... I'm a coward."

"No, you're a survivor," Cookie corrected, shoving up to standing. "That's what you are."

He rounded the table then and pulled her up to her feet. She staggered a little as he yanked her along, not sure what was happening. In three steps they were at the storeroom door. Then without a word, he was shoving it open and pushing her out into the storm.

A flash of light filled the air. Thunder rumbled in the distance. The rain pelted them, falling down to soak their clothes.

But the thing was, Cookie didn't seem to feel it. He kept hold of her hand as he picked up his pace, practically jogging in front of her, pulling her along. By the time they crested the steep hill and reached the stone house, her hair was plastered to her head. Cookie still didn't stop. He didn't stop until they were inside the front door, surrounded by all the men, dripping water onto the newly installed wood floor.

"What in the hell?" Cole spat and everything stopped.

Everything and everyone paused in their hammering and cutting, in their measuring and arguing. All eyes swiveled over to them and Cookie just pulled her around in front of him and gave her a gentle nudge.

"Tell them," he commanded. "Tell them what you just told me."

CHAPTER TWENTY-ONE_
COLE

THE NOISE LEVEL WAS OFF THE CHARTS. EVERYONE WAS shouting at once and right in the middle of it, Hannah... *his* Hannah, was trembling like a leaf. Cookie had dragged her through the storm. She was soaked through, looking every bit like a drowned cat. But the story she had just told them, well it was like lighting a stick of dynamite inside a fireworks factory.

"How many were there?" Someone shouted again.

"Men or women?" Hannah's voice shook.

"Women."

"Just the one," she confirmed.

"Are you sure?"

"Yes..." Hannah hesitated. "But I didn't see inside the building."

"So, there could be more?"

"I don't know."

They had questioned her like this three times already.

And every time they did it, the answers they got weren't enough. Cole had to put a stop to it. He had to end it soon. She was getting worn down. He could see it in the way her body shivered. She was trying so hard to give them what they wanted but he needed to make them stop.

"That's enough." Cole stepped in finally, raising a hand. Walking up close to her, he used his body to shield her from view.

The others grumbled and circled around, talking amongst themselves. Talking against him. Yeah, Cole had heard the rumors. Cookie had been whispering in his ear for weeks. He knew they wanted to leave, knew he had lost their respect. And truthfully, he couldn't blame them. Not really.

They just wanted a chance at a life, a *real* life, which included the possibility of a woman, maybe kids, a family like before. Not even the guarantee of one, just the possibility. But Cole refused to give them that. Now Cookie had delivered it lock stock and barrel. It made him wonder how much of the story was true.

"Hey," Cole whispered to her, smoothing back the wet hair from her face. "You okay? You're cold. We should get you warmed up, out of these wet clothes."

"I'm fine." Hannah looked up at him, worry etched clearly in the lines of her face.

"No, you're definitely not fine," Cole corrected, catching her chin in his hand. "Did Cookie put you up to this?"

"What?" Hannah stepped back from him. "No, I know what I saw."

"Then why haven't you ever told me?"

"Because I was ashamed," Hannah answered. "And you never asked."

His mouth dropped a moment before snapping shut. *Because you never asked.* The sentence was like a bomb in his mind. There were so many things he wanted to ask her, needed to ask her, but he hadn't done it. He was respecting her space, building trust, trying not to push her too hard before she was ready.

The frustrated energy that pulsed through him had him pacing away from her. All this time, the marks were there, staring him in the face, and he could have simply asked about them? Stopping in his tracks, his eyes sought Chan across the room. He and Liam were the only two people Cole had told about the marks. But only Chan knew why it was such a big deal.

The code. The orders from Command. Chan's assignment to kill Cole. Now here Hannah was with the code written on her back, only it was practically indecipherable. He needed Chan to look at it but he hadn't had the guts to ask her.

Maybe he really *was* losing his edge. Maybe he really didn't deserve to lead this unit any longer.

"Can you take us back there?" Davey resumed questioning her.

"I think so," Hannah confirmed.

"We should start getting ready," Ryder spoke out. "We could leave tomorrow."

"Wait-" Cole broke in. "It's the beginning of winter, the rains have come and soon there will be snow. You can't prepare for an assault like this in twenty-four hours."

"Every day we waste is another day that woman is suffering," Trey pointed out. "I agree with Ryder, we need to get out of here by tomorrow."

"Listen, this isn't the way to plan an op," Cole argued. "You're going in blind. You're going to get yourselves killed."

"I think we just disagree," Ryder piped up again. "We've got more skin in this game than you."

Cole opened his mouth to speak. He opened it to try to talk sense to them but they had already dismissed him. They had already turned away. If they left this compound tomorrow, low on ammo, low on food, then their chances of making it back were cut substantially.

And if they thought for one second they were leaving here like that with Hannah, then they had a fucking fight coming.

Beside him, Hannah was grabbing at his arm and pulling him back. Cole glanced down at her briefly, then up to the room. He was losing control. They would go whether he gave his consent or not. If his guys didn't make it back, then the compound wouldn't hold up much longer. Not without the full team. Not without their constant work and their protection.

"How long do you need to keep them here?" Hannah

asked, her voice low as they moved to the far corner of the room.

"What?" Cole's head was still reeling, he couldn't let them go like this. He wanted to help them, but he needed time to prepare.

"Cookie says you're losing your position." Hannah's eyes darted across his face. "They aren't going to listen to you because you won't share me."

"Han-"

"They have hope of finding more women now, but I only saw one. That's still not enough and she could already be dead." Hannah sucked in a breath. "How long do you need them to stay to prepare for this rescue?"

"I don't know. A week, maybe two."

"Then go tell them to stay and-"

"I tried," Cole cut in.

"Tell them to stay *and* while you prepare for the rescue, then I'll choose one of them... you know, to share."

"What?" Cole's eye's narrowed as his stomach dropped through the floor.

"This place... how long will we be able to stay if they don't make it back?"

"Hannah..." Cole stammered. "No."

"How *long* will it be safe here if they don't come back?"

"I can't. I mean... I don't know," Cole admitted. "A few months maybe."

"Then go tell them you'll share me with one of them," Hannah hissed, a touch of desperation filtering through her words.

"I *cannot* do that, Han."

"If you don't do it, then they will leave." Hannah's eyes met his, held them. "You'll lose the guys first, then the compound and we'll be running again, just like with Andy. I'll get caught and you'll get killed."

"I'd never let that happen." Cole gripped her arms, shook her a little.

"Please, Cole. Please," Hannah pleaded with him, her eyes getting wide and glassy. "I'll end up just like that woman in the cage. Don't you do that to me, Cole. Please don't."

CHAPTER TWENTY-TWO_
LIAM

THE ANNOUNCEMENT CAME AS QUITE A SHOCK. COLE HAD been whispering with Hannah in the corner and the rest of the room was caught up and swirling at the news of another live woman. Ryder and Davey were already hashing out half-ass plans, with Trey adding in suggestions that had Liam rolling his eyes. This was going to be an absolute shit show.

Too many opinions. Not enough experience leading. It could be a bonafide blood bath.

But what else were they going to do? Cole had lost his credibility and even though half of them still wanted him to lead, the other half were louder and more committed. Whether Cole liked it or not, the team was going to be heading out, in the fucking rain, to slog their way to this woman, starting tomorrow.

Liam only hoped that Cookie would be able to prep enough on-the-go meals to last them. Then there was the issue of finding the damn place. Only Hannah knew where it was and that had been months ago in the dark... when it was dry.

She had wandered, by her own admission, aimlessly to that place and then run like a bat out of hell away from it. The chances of her being able to get them even close to it were questionable. But then again, for Liam, he only needed to be close. If he could just get a scent of them, the faintest hint, then he could track them. No question.

Then out of nowhere, Cole was standing in the middle of the room with Hannah tucked up neatly by his side. He cleared his throat and began to speak.

"I know some of you have lost confidence in me," Cole started, and the room quieted immediately at his admission. "You don't think I have it in me anymore. You forget what we've been through together, the sacrifices we've made.

There's been talk... and I've heard it. You think I'm only out for me now. You think I've put myself above you. And I get why you feel that way, really I do. But all this time while I was losing your respect, I was working to build some trust, somewhere else."

Cole paused, his hand still clasped tightly around Hannah's. He looked down at her and everyone's eyes followed his. She was trembling just a little. She had changed into Cole's dry shirt but her pants were still dripping water onto the floor. Liam thought she couldn't get any more beautiful.

She nodded at Cole then, her head tilted up, giving him the signal to continue... and so he did.

Liam could tell his oldest friend wasn't sure about this. It was in the way Cole's jaw tightened almost imperceptibly and the way his fingers danced along the back of Hannah's hand. But these were subtle tells. Tells Liam himself had only learned because they had grown up together. To the rest of the crew, he looked deadly calm.

"But now I've got that trust, and it's time to prove to you all that I still have the team's best interest at heart. It's time to prove to you that when I tell you it will take two weeks to plan this next op, that it will take *exactly* two weeks to plan this op.

I have your back. I put you first. I always will. So, while we work to make this thing happen, Hannah is going to meet with you all, one on one. And before we go, she will..."

Cole swallowed then, his eyes darting across the faces of the crew. Liam stood transfixed to the spot, just like everyone else was. He couldn't hardly believe what he was hearing... and he didn't want to do a thing to stop it.

"She will be choosing another one of you to spend her nights with."

Liam's jaw dropped.

Well that was one way to put it, he thought. Hannah was taking on another lover.

CHAPTER TWENTY-THREE_
HANNAH

"FIRST THINGS FIRST," COLE WAS SAYING. "WE NEED YOU TO tell us about the marks."

"Marks?" Hannah's face scrunched up in confusion. *What was he talking about?*

They were still in the stone house, though many hours had passed. Someone had lit a fire in the new fireplace and it was spreading its warmth throughout the half finished space. Hannah was sitting on a chair, it was the only one Davey had completed so far. Putting a hand up to her forehead, she closed her eyes.

Was it possible to be any more tired than this? And it wasn't just physically. She had been that, been that a thousand times over. It was the emotional aspect. Hannah was utterly drained.

After the announcement, the one that Cole had absolutely not wanted to make, everything had changed. She could see it immediately. The guys were listening to him again, nodding their heads and settling back into them-selves. The growing desperation, the tense energy from before, it had dissipated, then it was gone altogether.

He had them back now. All of them. They were a cohe-sive unit again and Cole was once more at the head. Hannah knew she had to do everything in her power to keep him there. Everything.

"Come on Han." Cole stepped closer to her. He was agitated, she could tell. "The ones on your back. The code."

"I..." Hannah blanched, the color draining from her face. "I have something on my back?"

She twisted in her seat, grabbing at the collar of her shirt as if she could actually see for herself. Was it possi-ble? Andy had never mentioned it and he didn't have anything on his body. Not marks or code, or whatever that was.

Code is a special kind of writing. The thought came to her in an instant, but it didn't match up to anything else in her mind. Hannah's hands began to shake. Something was truly wrong with her. She was crazy.

Turning back to them, she watched Cole's glance shoot to Chan who frowned. Liam stood a bit off to one side. His dark eyes were staring at her, making her feel... she didn't know what. Involuntarily, her body heated. She pressed her palms to her cheeks and looked away.

It was only the four of them left in the house. The others had finally gone after a full day spent inside together, planning. Cole handed out the assignments the way he usually did and thankfully no one had batted an eye, or raised a question. It further solidified Hannah's resolve to see this thing through.

Over the next two weeks, Cookie and Hannah would be doing meal prep and packing. Ace, Ryder and Chan would be selecting weapons and ammo, cleaning and distributing them.

Trey and Davey would sort through their gear, making sure everyone had the right stuff to hike for days, possibly weeks, in winter conditions. They would also be responsible for figuring out how to transport the woman back home if the mission was successful. Liam and Cole would be working with Hannah to pinpoint the location. But Liam would be doing the tracking.

"You didn't tell me about the woman because I didn't ask, right?" Cole's voice was controlled, his eyes darting over her face. "So, I'm asking now. I'm asking about the Command Code on your back. Did you work for them? Were you a soldier? How did you make it up here? Are you on a mission?"

"No." Hannah shook her head, feeling at once there had been a mistake. She had no idea what he was talking about. But then she hesitated and her eyes shifted from Cole to Chan and then over to Liam. "I mean... I don't know."

"You don't know?" Cole's voice was incredulous.

"I don't know!" Hannah shouted it before shoving out of her chair.

Silence filled the room.

Frustrated and frightened, she walked first to the fire place, then drew a ragged breath. Standing still in front of it, Hannah watched the flames leap and dance. The heat was so mesmerizing. It was beautiful and hot and she wanted to disappear into it all of a sudden.

Dropping her eyes to the scar on her right hand, she brushed her thumb over it. There were so many unanswered questions. She was backed into a corner now.

With a huff, she crossed to one of the windows next and looked out of it. The glass was smooth, divided into four equal squares, another relic from "the farmhouse" that so bothered Cole. If he got to keep that to himself, then why did she have to confess this to them?

Because Cole asked and you want him to protect you. Hannah sighed. There was no getting around it.

"I've never heard of Command Code," Hannah spoke to the window at first.

Rotating around slowly, she leaned back against the windowsill and crossed her arms instinctively over her chest. "But that doesn't mean I wasn't a soldier, or whatever you say. I just don't remember anything past about eight or nine months ago. I don't know what's on my back, I've never seen it."

Cole huffed a laugh at first, running one hand back through his shaggy chestnut hair. Chan was reserved, as he usually was, not giving away the thoughts that surely passed through his head. But Liam. Hannah's eyes found his and what she saw there made her wonder. He believed her.

When Cole took a step towards her, his energy all frustrated, getting ready to say something else, Liam stuck out a hand and stopped him. He gave his head a slight shake as he looked at his friend and had Cole's brow furrowing. Though the communication between them was silent, the two men spoke to one another just the same. Hannah waited.

"Will you let us see your back?" Cole asked finally, and Hannah nodded.

She turned away from them, pulling up on the bottom of her shirt as she again faced the window. Well, it was one of Cole's shirts really. Her soaked clothes were spread out on the floor by the fire, drying out. Someone had brought her an extra set of dry pants and she had already slipped into them. Actually it was Liam who had brought them to her. She recalled the way Cole had glanced up and mumbled a thank you as Liam handed them over. His dark hair had been all wet from the rain.

Removing her shirt completely, Hannah swallowed hard and held it against her bare chest. For a moment, the men behind her seemed frozen in place. No one moved. No one said anything. After a beat, she pulled her hair aside to reveal all of her back, then glanced over her shoulder at them.

Liam sucked in a breath and looked down. Cole and Chan approached her, eyes locked on her back. When they got close, they both reached out. She could feel their fingertips brush softly down her spine, then back up. They were murmuring to one another, so focused on whatever was written there. The marks.

Craning her neck as far as it would go, Hannah tried to

see too, but only managed to glimpse the very last length of her back where it met her butt. There was nothing there.

"Have you tried reading it upside down?" Chan asked.

"Yes." Cole nodded his head. "It's even more nonsense that way."

Hannah frowned then, wondering when he had a chance to read it. Then it dawned on her, Cole had studied the marks while she slept. She felt a touch of betrayal work its way into her blood stream and begin to simmer. Turning her face back to the window, she felt her cheeks flush but worked to keep her breathing regular, controlled.

"What could have made this?" Liam's voice was close now.

He had crept over without her noticing and all at once she felt his fingers brush against her skin. It sent gooseflesh blooming.

"I've never seen anything like it," Chan answered. "But it's solid, definitely not something done by hand. Do you see how straight these lines are? And the blocks, the sizing of them is perfect. It had to be from a stamp or template, maybe done by a computer."

"Computer?" Cole spoke now, Hannah glanced back again and watched him rub the scruff of his chin. "So it had to be done during the war, the early stages maybe. But why? How is it that color?"

"Bleaching?" Chan suggested. "Maybe a special kind of laser? I don't think we'll ever know for sure."

"Unless she remembers," Liam suggested.

All of their eyes bounced up to hers then, only just

seeming to remember she was standing there, that the marks they were studying were on her body. Hannah blinked at them a few times and they watched her with varying degrees of scrutiny.

"I've tried to remember, but I can't," she said finally.

"That's alright." Liam was quick to step in. "You will."

"Yeah," Cole agreed after a beat, his eyes flicking again to Chan. "It's okay Han. Just let us look a bit longer, okay?"

"Okay."

"Do we have anything to write on?" Chan asked. "It would be easier to play around with it that way. Try different combinations and such."

"What, you mean like pen and paper?" Cole gave a short laugh. "No man, nothing like that."

"You could carve it out," Liam suggested. "On the walls or floor."

"That would work," Chan again. "Got a knife on you?"

"You have to ask?"

Hannah watched Liam hand over a long shining blade which Chan took before crouching down. Her neck began to ache from twisting to watch them so she sighed and straightened.

Outside, the darkness had come and the rain had let up. The window pane was still streaked with a few remaining drops but she was able to make out the silhouettes of towering trees. Just above them, a few clouds shifted across a moonlit sky. Moving quickly, the clouds were pushed by a strong wind, one that howled as it passed over the stone house in the night.

LK MAGILL

She heard scratching against the wood, then every once in a while, Cole would murmur something. After that he would stand and point to a spot on her back, sometimes touching her, sometimes just hovering above her skin. At one point, Liam strode away and threw more wood on the fire. The light in the room was waning and they needed to see her better.

"So, I think it's mirror writing," Chan announced finally.

"What's that?" Liam asked.

"Like its flipped around," Chan tried to explain. "Did you ever have writing on your shirt and then stand in front of a mirror? When you try to read the words they are flipped around, not backwards, but each letter is the wrong direction. I think the code stamped on her is reversed like that. The marks are each backwards, but not out of order."

"Holy shit," Cole's eyes lit as Hannah turned to look at them. "You're right."

Quick as anything Cole snatched the knife from Chan and began to copy the marks down again. As he worked, Chan talked.

"It's like a bar code," he explained. "If I had a scanner with me, then I could capture the marks and they would flip around and then I'd read them the correct way on the display."

"Done," Cole announced, and the men all stood and stepped back.

Hannah pulled the shirt back over her head and then rotated around. Gazing down at the marks in the wooden floor, both she and Liam were still at a loss. He was scratching his head with a look of confusion on his face.

The marks were a series of squares, lines, dashes and dots. They were grouped together in places, then spread apart in others. The entire thing was in the shape of a single long column, about two inches wide and maybe twelve inches long.

"Well?" Liam demanded. "What the hell does it say?"

"It includes a lot of abbreviations," Chan explained. "So some of it would still be open to interpretation."

"Give me the exact translation first," Liam prompted.

"F. Loc 7. NA. A @ Year Zero..." Chan recited until Liam cut him off.

"Alright, alright, I get it. It's beyond me." Liam slashed his hand through the air as Cole crouched, hands bracing either side of his face, reading the marks on the floor. "So, what's it all mean?"

"They're stats," Chan said, and Cole nodded slowly.

"Female. Location 7. North America. Age at Year Zero: 19. Genetic Abnormalities: None Present. Breeding: Phase 3. Name: Hannah M. Linfield. Population Number: 11681."

HE SHOULDN'T HAVE PUSHED HER SO HARD. HE SHOULD HAVE stopped the questioning sooner. But the revelations on her back just swept Cole away. Why was it that when he focused on the right things for Hannah, the team suffered, and when he focused on being a good leader, Hannah suffered?

This balance thing was not his strong suit. Cole was all focus, all drive, all the time. That was part of the reason why, during two years of fighting, they had only lost four guys. And all of them had died during that last mission, the one where his head wasn't completely in the game.

And it had all been Cole's fault. He had been distracted, knowing that at the end, Chan would have to kill him. Because that was the order he had received, and that was the plan the two of them had agreed to.

It was what they had promised to do as they sat together in the dark, with the bombs raining down outside of that abandoned suburb. It was the commitment they had made while the crew slept in the master bedroom of some poor dead family's house, and Chan tried not to pass out.

But even then, Cole had been adamant. *We burn the building, take out the target, and then you just turn and do it*, he had said. But Chan shook his head, looking pale.

You're not a double agent, Chan had pleaded. Cole could still hear the strain in his voice.

It will be just you and me, Cole reminded him. *Put a bullet in my head and tell the others it was enemy fire.*

Chan's head just kept shaking slowly side to side, then he dashed to the bathroom and proceed to throw up... again. It wasn't that Chan was a weak man, he wasn't. Hell, Cole had witnessed him kill well over a hundred soldiers in their time together.

But there was something about having to kill your buddy; an undeserving one at that. It turned your insides sour, made you question what the hell you were doing at all. If Chan didn't follow through though, then the team would never be able to return to Command.

None of them could ever go back. They could never take another mission. They would all have to defect. They would all have to run. And Cole figured that was a death sentence in itself so he was willing to be the one to go first.

Cole would die in order for the team to have a chance at long term survival. And by the morning, Chan had agreed. It was all settled.

But then they were both standing in the enemy's office with the opposition's commander bleeding out on the floor. It was just him and Chan. The crew was outside, setting fires and executing soldiers before getting the hell out of there.

Just do it, Cole had hissed, but he couldn't quite keep the tremble from his voice. He really didn't want to die.

I can't. Chan's hand shook as he held his weapon, like actually side to side big time shook.

For a minute, maybe more, Cole waited. He kept his eyes on the floor, listening to the crackle of the team giving status updates on the headsets in their helmets. Still, Chan didn't pull the trigger.

You can't wait any longer, Cole said finally. *You've got to get the team out of here, they're exposed.*

Again, nothing. Chan kept the gun pointed at Cole's face and the two of them just stared at one another.

The seconds felt like hours. Sweat was beading on Cole's upper lip and dripping in slow lines from his forehead. If the headsets hadn't lit up just then, if the crew hadn't begun chiming and shouting, then maybe Chan and Cole would have just burned to death in that building together. Maybe that had been Chan's ultimate compromise all along.

But suddenly it wasn't about Cole or Chan anymore. Suddenly it was about four guys left exposed for too long without a leader to tell them what to do. And by the time Chan and Cole left the office, running down the hall, screaming orders into their headsets, it was too late.

Four of their brothers had died that day instead of Cole. And he would never, *ever* forgive himself.

"I'm sorry," Cole whispered the words out loud even though Hannah couldn't hear him.

She was fast asleep, snuggled up next to him on the narrow mattress in his cabin. It was warm. The fire was still burning well and the space was so small that it didn't need a lot of wood to keep it comfortable. Cole lay on his back, one hand wrapped around her. He pressed his lips to her hair, then exhaled a breath.

He had kept her in the stone house with him all day after their big announcement, the thought of which still made his gut twist. The crew had set to work planning for the rescue. He should've walked Hannah back to the cabin then. He should've brought her food and let her rest. But instead, he made her stay late into the night, until only Liam and Chan were left.

They were the only two people he trusted with the information about the marks on Hannah's back and he needed them there when he confronted her. Thinking back, he was still in awe. It had practically knocked him over when she told him she couldn't remember anything beyond the past half year or so of her life.

He hadn't believed her at first, hadn't wanted to. But then Liam had given him that look and as usual it made Cole think twice.

That was the way it had always been between them. Liam observed while Cole went all out. And Cole had needed that check from his friend, was downright glad to have him back on his side. For a moment there, in the chaos before the announcement, he had worried Liam would be leaving with the others. They had all certainly crowded around him, trying to convince him of their plans.

But a chance at having Hannah, and a promise to rescue this other woman, had changed everything. Even Cole had to admit that. Though thinking about the consequences made him squeamish and angry in turns. Sharing Hannah, the thought made him positively sick.

Running his hand up her back, Cole pulled her closer against his body, and she let out a tiny sigh. It brought a flood of relief to him. She was really okay.

They had all been standing there, debating what the marks on her back meant. There was a population of people with code on them, maybe more than eleven-thousand. And there were "location centers"... at least seven. The revelations kept pouring over them and it was an adrenaline hit to the heart.

But then there were things they couldn't quite figure out. What was Year Zero? Hannah looked older than nineteen, like by four or five years maybe. And then there was the stuff about genetics and breeding phases. They had started to question her and that's when Cole should've seen it. It was too much.

"Hannah M. Linfield." Cole read her full name off of the wooden floor, then looked up to analyze her face. "Does that ring a bell for you?"

"I'm sorry." Hannah ran a hand through her hair before giving a slight shake of her head. "No."

"You don't remember anything? None of this?" Cole gestured to the marks, though he knew she couldn't read them. "Where were you living when you got the code?"

Cole watched her then as she continued to shake her head, and the tears began to well in her eyes. She had been so worn out, why hadn't he seen it? But he was suddenly so close to something, Cole could hardly name it.

For the past three years there hadn't been any further contact from Command. They never saw anymore fighters, not ones like them. When they'd defected, they took nothing along that had any electronics. They'd ditched their helmets with the headsets, ripped the GPS bullshit off their rifles.

Chan had destroyed the scanner and left it in the dirt down south as Cole watched. So there hadn't been any way to get more code even if Command had tried to send it. And of course there was nothing left of humanity by that point anyway. No women. No children. No civilization. Only death and the bare minimum of survival.

But now. Well, now it was like a whole other part of the story was standing in front of them, but they didn't have any way to get it. It was locked inside Hannah, with no way out.

Cole had taken a step closer to her then, still not really seeing Hannah before that moment. His eyes narrowed, it was like he finally woke up. Her chest was heaving, she was working to suck in air and her eyes were wide. Confusion and fear contorted her features and though she tried like hell, she wasn't getting any oxygen.

Before Cole could react, her eyes had rolled up in the back of her head and she passed out. He was a terrible boyfriend, or whatever he was to her. He should have stopped it way before that, he should have seen.

Thank God Liam was fast though. His oldest friend had stepped in, and where Cole failed to react quickly enough, Liam was able to catch Hannah before her head hit the floor.

CHAPTER TWENTY-FIVE_
HANNAH

HER BOOTS LEFT TRACKS IN THE MUD AS SHE FLED THE warmth of the stone house and made her way down the hillside. The sky was bright overhead, a perfect shade of vibrant blue and the sun, it was shining. Soon the mud would be all dried up, that is if the shock of pleasant weather were to hold.

Cole had been hovering all morning. He'd insisted she accompany him everywhere he went, and though she understood why he was feeling extra protective, she knew it had to come to an end.

When Hannah had fainted the night before, the look of worry and guilt that filled Cole's face was the first thing she saw when she came to. It wasn't his fault, and though she tried to tell him that, he just wouldn't listen. That was the thing about Cole, Hannah realized, he had a one track mind.

That was what made him so great for this place and so

great for this team. He was able to see the end goal and did everything in his power to get there. Even if it meant he had to drag everyone behind in his wake. People were easily swept up by his confidence and the results were undeniable.

She appreciated that about him, really she did, but when Cole's focus suddenly fell directly on her, Hannah knew he was blind to everything else. Blind to the fact that she had to spend time with the rest of the team... without him around.

So when Cookie sent her to the storeroom to begin work on meal prep, she bobbed her head and was out the solid wood door before Cole had a chance to protest. The air felt good, all crisp and clear, washed clean by the storm. Quite a few branches had been knocked to the ground and Hannah had to sidestep more than one in her effort to reach the fire pit.

Her hands were overflowing with clean dishes from the crew's breakfast. They still didn't have enough shelf space to keep them at the stone house and so she was forced to carry them back and forth. The tower they made in her hands was awkward and heavy and she had to crane her neck in order to see the path before her. Suddenly her foot began to slip and she would have gone down, but someone caught her elbow and held her upright.

"Whoa, there." Davey smiled. "Looks like you've got your hands full."

"Hey." Hannah smiled up at him, she hadn't noticed him following her. "Thanks."

"Where're you headed?" Davey asked, as he began to take dishes from her, stacking them in his own arms. "Can I help?"

"Um, the storeroom," Hannah answered, her nerves churning. She reminded herself that this was the idea. She had to spend time with each of them over the next two weeks, might as well start now. "I'd love the help."

"Great."

Now free of any burden, Hannah let her hands twist together in front of her as they both picked their way down to the clearing. Even though the stone house was still under construction, Cookie was halfway moved into it already. The fireplace worked and it was extra large. Davey had rigged it so that Cookie would be able to use it to make meals instead of the fire ring outside. He was handy that way, Davey was. It made Hannah smile.

"What?" Davey asked, looking down at her.

"You," she answered honestly.

"Me?" Davey looked surprised, then pleased.

She could tell he wanted more details, but she didn't offer any. Though her stomach did a little flip and her pulse quickened, Hannah couldn't help but think of Cole. She knew he didn't want this, and the knowledge put an edge on her.

Davey came to a stop at the storeroom door, and Hannah moved to open it for him. He grinned sheepishly then, holding it open with his foot and waited. She looked at him with a puzzled expression.

"I'm supposed to open the door for you," Davey supplied. "It's how we were raised."

"Oh." Hannah nibbled at her bottom lip as she quickly stepped over the threshold first. "Who's we?"

"Me and Ryder," Davey explained as he followed her. "He's my little brother."

"I didn't know that," Hannah commented.

As she turned to look at him, she noted his tousle of blonde hair and the sparkle of his blue eyes. They were echoed in Ryder, now that she thought about it.

Pointing to the shelf closest to the door, Hannah showed him where Cookie liked to keep everything. Davey held still as she unloaded cups, bowls, plates and silverware from his arms, putting each stack carefully in its proper place.

At first he asked her questions, did she have any siblings? Where did she grow up? What did she like to do? But Hannah was forced to deflect, not able to come up with any truthful answers. Sure, Cole and Liam and Chan all knew her secret, but she wasn't ready to share it with anyone else.

Gesturing for him to sit at the little work table, Hannah quickly began asking questions of her own. As she gathered the supplies necessary for making the team's on-the-go meals, she listened to Davey talk.

He was four years older than Ryder. They were both raised by a single dad, his mom had died of cancer when he was ten. He loved a game called hockey, was from a place called Wisconsin, and made a joke she didn't understand about cheese.

He was an easy companion, Hannah realized. Eager to help with the array of food and happy to talk when she so obviously wasn't. Glancing up at him occasionally, Hannah realized how much Davey smiled. He had nice straight white teeth, and they flashed at her often. He was pleasant to look at, his eyes were extra pretty and nothing about him seemed forced.

They probably would have gone on that way all day except Cookie came in and spoiled the mood.

"You're not doing it right." Cookie hovered over Davey and let out an exasperated breath. "The portions are too big. No, no, no. You can't cut em' down *that* small."

At a loss, Davey laughed out loud and pushed the chair back. He gave Hannah a knowing wink before dusting off his jacket and pushing out the door.

"I thought he'd never leave," Cookie spat, then took Davey's place at the table.

"You chased him off, Cookie," Hannah scolded him, but there was no malice in it.

"Damn straight I did." Cookie nodded and reached out to continue cutting up the dried mutton.

Hannah noted that the pieces were exactly the same size Davey had been making them. She shook her head at him and stuck her tongue in her cheek. Cookie had some personality to spare, and she loved every bit of it.

"Listen here, Little Miss," Cookie began, eyes darting behind her to the closed door. "You and I need to have a talk before the line of idiots out there starts busting down the door."

"Oh?" Hannah turned to look. The exaggeration was not lost on her, but she simply *had* to bait him.

"Well, they aren't all there right this minute," Cookie hissed, then realized his mistake when Hannah turned to smile at him. "Oh, you're a sly one. That's good. That's what I thought."

Hannah waited a beat for him to continue, but he just looked at her a moment, appraising. Though she enjoyed these little exchanges with him, Hannah's patience was wearing a bit thin, so she rolled her eyes and returned to her cutting.

"Go on, Cookie," she prompted finally.

"I told them this was my turn to spend time with you," he announced, then added. "But you can take me out of the running, I've had enough of women to last a lifetime."

Hannah's hands stilled and her eyebrows shot up with surprise. This was the first she had heard of Cookie's past and she suddenly realized she wanted to know more about him. How had he become the man he was now? How did he get to be with a team of guys half his age? They all respected him so much. What had he done to earn that respect?

But she would be disappointed once again. He would give her no more than that.

"So you don't want to take me on as a lover?" Hannah asked quietly, her lips quirking at the look of annoyance that crossed his face.

"No dear," he said. "No offense, of course."

"Then what are we doing here, Cookie? Why did you kick Davey out?"

"Davey." Cookie tapped his fingers on the table. "He's a nice boy, isn't he?"

"Yes, he seems nice."

"I'd say he's in the top three," Cookie commented.

"What are you trying to say?" Hannah stopped what she was doing and gave Cookie her undivided attention.

He was usually so candid that this subtle discussion was a bit unnerving. Clearly, he had something to say but he was being very measured in his delivery, which wasn't like him. That combined with her memory issues left her feeling at a loss.

"I watched you in that room yesterday." Cookie gestured behind him in the direction of the far stone house. "When Cole was losing his influence and the team was splitting, *you* are the one that stitched it all back together. It wasn't Cole's idea to share you. It was yours."

"It was," Hannah admitted.

"I could play coy and ask you why, but I think we both know the truth."

"And what's that?"

"You're a sleeper."

"I'm sorry?" Hannah huffed a laugh. She had no idea what he meant.

"A sleeper," Cookie confirmed. "You work behind the scenes but in reality you're running the whole show."

"I am not," Hannah countered. She'd only done what Cookie himself had suggested. Hadn't she?

"You are."

"I only did what you said," Hannah argued. "Cole was losing his position because he wouldn't share me. So I made him share."

"To keep him in power… the man *you're* sleeping with."

Hannah sucked in a breath and looked away. Was that why she'd done it? She shook her head, it wasn't that simple.

"If Cole isn't the leader, the team will split…" Hannah tried to explain herself.

"Quite frankly, I don't care why you want him in power. The only thing that matters is that I want him there, too."

"Why?"

"That's not the issue." Cookie spread his palms out on the table, pushing aside pieces of meat and tools as he went. "What matters now is the next man you pick to sleep with."

"I don't understand."

"Come on, Little Miss." He frowned at her. "You can't pick just anyone. You've got to pick the one that is the biggest threat to Cole and neutralize it."

"Threat?" Hannah's heart began to pound inside her chest. "Someone's threatening him?"

"Not like that," Cookie clarified. "Not threatening his person, threatening his position. If the team were to split… who would they choose to lead them? If they had gone on that rescue mission without Cole, what man would they most want to go with them?"

"You want me to choose the second leader."

"I want you to choose the man that the rest of them would be afraid to leave without. The one they want fighting alongside them, the one that would help them most to survive. If you pick that man and make it so he'll never want to leave you, then the rest of them will never be able to go either."

"Who is it?" Hannah was breathless, her heart had only increased in its pace.

"Like I said," Cookie leaned back. "Davey is in the top three."

CHAPTER TWENTY-SIX_
LIAM

IT LOOKED GOOD, IT WAS DONE. SO WHY DID HE KEEP obsessing over it? Liam sat at his workbench, the door to his shop hanging open, a cold breeze blowing in from outside. The little bracelet shined in the palm of his hand as his eyes checked over the design again.

He had forged each small link out of metal before etching tiny flowers into it. Then he had buffed and smoothed the damn thing until it shone in the daylight and the darkness alike. As if that wasn't enough, he then re-carved the pattern deeper and repeated the entire process.

But it was done now. It had to be.

She would be meeting with him any day. Practically everyone else had spent their time with her already. He tried not to let the order of Hannah's choosing bother him. He just hoped he wasn't the last one. It meant she was avoiding him, though he couldn't blame her really.

When she had first come to live with them he hadn't

exactly been welcoming. Damn it. He wished he could go back and be... *not* himself.

Shoving back from his stool, Liam left the bracelet on his worktable and stepped outside. The sun had held for the past ten days but another storm was moving in. From this vantage point, he could see the dark clouds swirling in the distance. There was no denying what was headed their way. It would be a cold one too, the bite of wind was a warning. The temperature had dropped considerably over the past twenty-four hours.

Snow. They would have snow just in time for the rescue mission. Liam grimaced at the thought. It would cover up their target's tracks.

Eyes scanning, he dropped his gaze to the fire ring and noted the handful of men lingering there. Ryder, Chan and Ace. They had given him their knives a while back to look over and sharpen before the impending mission. Since Hannah had met with all of them already, he might as well jog down there and deliver the weapons. They wouldn't be doing anything else for a bit.

Glancing past them hopefully he was forced to huff out a breath when he didn't see her anywhere. This waiting thing was driving him nuts.

Shoving into his cabin, he stepped to his new desk and pulled open one of the drawers. Yeah, Davey wasn't the only one who could be handy, Liam thought. He wasn't the only one who could build furniture. Inside the drawer were the completed knives, each tucked neatly into their worn leather sheaths.

Gathering them up, Liam spun on his heel and took a quick, if not neurotic, survey of his home. The full size mattress was up on a bed frame now, pushed into the far corner. A few blankets were spread over it with his sleeping bag rolled up neatly to serve as a long pillow.

He had swept the floor, he didn't know how many times, and there was a chair positioned in the other corner. Along the wall, he had installed a series of low wooden shelves that served as a sort of dresser for him. His clothes were still folded and sorted how Hannah had done it that first time.

Running one large hand down his face, Liam let loose a groan. What the hell was he doing? He wasn't this guy anymore. He wasn't that guy still in college. The one who would never have slit someone's throat. The one who would never have done unspeakable things to countless soldiers all because the man above him told him to.

"She's never going to pick you," Liam spoke into the silence before backing outside and shutting the door.

He didn't deserve her, he knew that better than anyone. He was too much like his father. Too fucking much, and bloodlines don't lie, right? That's what the bastard had always said anyway.

Plus, she was scared of him besides. They all were to a certain extent. Everyone except for Cole. In the past, Liam had liked it that way.

Picking his way down the hillside, Liam stopped at the fire beside the other guys. Ace and Chan gave him a nod. Ryder smiled. They were chit-chatting, hands held up to the flames, warming themselves in between tasks Cole had dished out.

"Here you go, fellas," Liam announced, handing them each their knife in turn.

They all nodded appreciatively, accepting their weapons back before taking them out of their sheaths to examine them. Chan ran his finger down the blade, feeling the edge before he smiled broadly.

"I can never get it this sharp, man."

"Me either, bro." Ace gave his a toss. "Perfect."

"Any pointers?" Ryder's eyes danced as he balanced the blade on the tip of his finger.

Fucking comedian, Liam thought. He genuinely liked Ryder, aside from the constant yammering. But the kid did leave himself a little too exposed when he went hand-to-hand. Might be a good chance for a quick lesson. Maybe even one inspired by the little spitfire herself.

Liam's eyes gleamed then, but Ryder didn't notice until it was too late. Moving fast as anything, Liam closed the distance between them, swiped Ryder's own knife off of his palm and drew it across the kid's throat. It was only the handle side of course, same as Hannah had done, but it scared the living shit out of everyone.

Ryder staggered back, hands clutching at his throat and the other's eyes went wide, mouths dropping in horror. Liam stepped away and began to chuckle. He couldn't help himself. Soon he was laughing and laughing, the way Cole had done.

So this was how Hannah felt when she had fake-stabbed him in the back. The look on his face must have been priceless, he realized.

"You are one cold mother-fucker." Chan's voice was ragged, but after he managed to collect himself, he started laughing, too.

"You should've seen the look on your face!" Ace was pointing at Ryder, then clutching at his own throat, staggering back in mock simulation.

"You got me," Ryder admitted. "You got me."

Pulling back his hands, the kid was staring at them in disbelief, so sure he should be seeing blood there. After a beat, he glanced over at Liam with a look of awe in his eyes.

"You've got to teach me," he demanded.

"Alright," Liam agreed, straightening. "You leave yourself too exposed whenever you lose your gun. We should start there."

Shrugging out of their jackets, he and Ryder began to spar. He put the kid through his paces and over the next hour, the two of them wore each other out. By the time he was done, a few more of the guys had gathered round, taking bets and heckling. For a moment, Liam forgot their circumstances. They were just a bunch of rowdy guys, playing at being tough. All they needed was a case of beer.

But then it all changed. He knew the moment *she* walked up. He could feel it in the air. Everything tensed, or everyone that is. Hannah's presence had always caused a stir but now that they were all under scrutiny, the pressure had increased.

Stepping back, Liam separated from Ryder who couldn't help the grin that spread across his youthful face. He was so freaking innocent, it was almost painful to watch.

"Hey guys, how's it going?" Hannah's voice was sweet and soft.

Her hair swirled around her face in the wind and she gave a little laugh as she brushed it back over her shoulder. The others all responded verbally, but Liam couldn't manage more than a nod. Anything he tried to say to her always came out harsh and short. He figured it was better just to keep his mouth shut altogether.

Cole skirted a few of the guys and went to give her a hug but she simply smiled at him and backed away. At first his friend frowned, but then Hannah wagged her finger teasingly at him and nibbled on her lower lip the way she always did. Her lips, they drove Liam to distraction.

"Ah, ah, ah," Hannah said and had them all chuckling appreciatively. "I was hoping Trey could help me sew up a few more food bags in the stone house."

"Sure thing." Trey practically jumped to her side.

Liam's stomach sank, and he tried not to watch them walk away together. Turns out he would be the last one she met with after all. It wasn't a good sign.

Some of the other guys came up to him and started asking more questions about the impending rescue. What did he think of the plan? What would he change? Did he think he could track them? Even in the snow?

He answered them at first, but his mind was off somewhere else. Off with Hannah, a woman he could never have. The only one he had ever wanted quite like this.

"We're going to need you to butcher that lamb," Cookie said, interrupting his thoughts. "*Before* the mission."

He had come out of nowhere, the old grump, suddenly materializing to stand in front of Liam, blinking expectantly. It was unusual for anyone to sneak up on him, so Liam did a double take. He had been so absorbed with Hannah, it left him feeling off his game.

"I just slaughtered that ewe two weeks ago," Liam reminded him. "She should last all winter."

"This rescue changes things," Cookie countered. "We've got six guys and a woman traipsing through the snow for weeks potentially. That's way more calories than usual. We need the lamb, too."

"I thought we agreed to save him for next year," Liam protested.

He really didn't want to butcher the lamb. There was just something about killing the livestock that was a challenge for him. It wasn't something he shared with anyone. Hell, they probably wouldn't understand. They had seen him do way worse to actual human beings without batting an eye.

But in some twisted way Liam had convinced himself that the men were deserving of what he did to them. The livestock, well... Liam took care of them. They depended on him, and though it was necessary for the team's survival, it was a sad sort of pain to take their lives. He would do it, though. He always did his job.

"That was then, this is now," Cookie quipped, and had Liam rolling his eyes.

"Sure thing old man, I'll go do it this instant."

"Not right now," Cookie amended. "Tomorrow morning. I've got to get the fat cut fresh off the meat for a new batch of soap and I don't have time for it tonight."

"Fine." Liam sighed. He didn't know why he ever fought with the wiry fucker, there was no point to it. "First light then, I'm not going to wait around all day."

"Wake me before you go down," Cookie commanded, then walked away.

The rest of the afternoon and into the evening, Liam waited for Hannah to come to him. She had finished with Trey and then disappeared into the storeroom for hours. When she emerged, she began carrying things up to the stone house for dinner.

Part of him wanted to follow her, to ask her when he would be getting a chance to speak to her. He wanted to show her his cabin and the changes he'd made. He wanted to give her the bracelet. But none of the others had to ask for their time, and he was afraid she might reject him outright.

So instead, he went about chopping wood, then slogged his way to dinner with the rest of the crew. The stone house was nearing completion. It had eight finished bunks, though no mattresses to go in them, a full length wooden table, shelves for Cookie's things, a few chairs and even a wide bench they could throw a sleeping bag on to make into a semi-comfortable couch.

They'd built the fireplace extra large so it kept the place plenty warm and with a few strategic candles and two lanterns set on shelves, the place was downright cheery, even in the dark of night.

At the long table, Hannah sat next to Cole. She was wedged between him and Davey and the look on her face was relaxed and happy, like she belonged there beside them. Between the flickering candle light and the hot meal of stew, the mood was turning rowdy and fun. Though Liam didn't share in the feeling, he did his best to play along.

Ace kept retelling the story of what Liam had done to poor Ryder, reenacting it with more exaggeration each time. The guys hooted and hollered until Ryder looked properly pissed and eventually Liam was forced to put a stop to it.

"Alright." Liam set down his water cup and the laughter died with it. "In Ryder's defense, I only learned that move from a certain woman who sits among you."

All eyes swiveled to Hannah, who met Liam's gaze for the first time that day. The comment alone was worth it just for that, Liam thought, with a small smile. After a beat, she blushed and looked down.

Cole, not seeming to notice, leaned forward and took over Ace's storytelling role. Before long everyone was laughing at Liam being stabbed in the back and Ryder's face relaxed.

She has to talk to me now, Liam thought, and his pulse kicked up a notch when she stood back from the table a few moments later. But instead of coming around to him and asking him to help her with the dishes, she announced she was tired and going to bed. It took all of Liam's willpower not to react. He kept his features calm, like he didn't give a shit, but the others were keeping track too so they stole glances at him regardless. He was being passed over tonight.

"I'll walk you," Cole volunteered, but then Cookie interfered.

"It's your turn to wash the dishes, Mr. High and Mighty." Cookie pointed at Cole with a stew covered spoon. "I'll accompany the lady to her suite."

And then off they went, out the door and into the night without so much as a backwards glance. After a beat of awkward silence, Ryder cracked some joke and the rest of them readily responded. They were all looking for a way to make it okay, to give Liam the space he needed. His jaw tightened and beneath the table he purposefully loosened his hand, opting to spread his fingers out rather than bunch them up. He had earned this from her, of that he had no doubt.

All the while that Cole went about washing dishes, Liam brooded. He watched his friend cross back and forth to the pot of hot water on the grate by the fire but he didn't really give him his full attention.

In his mind, Liam was reviewing all of the times he had ever interacted with Hannah and found himself properly shamed. He had been an asshole, yes, but wasn't there some way he could fix it? How could he get her to give him another chance? Maybe Cole could put in a good word for him. Yeah, his oldest friend was the only one who truly understood him. That was a good idea, right?

Liam's head shot up and swiveled around, searching for Cole, but he had already gone. *Shit. Shit. Shit. Shit.* Liam shoved back from the table, grabbed his coat from the hook by the door and pushed out into the night air.

It was dark, but clear. The clouds hadn't settled in yet. They had maybe another day before the storm. Glancing up, Liam noted the moon was full and the sky was scattered with a dusting of a million bright stars. He refocused his gaze down the hill towards Cole's cabin and spotted his friend's figure in the darkness, trudging steadily along.

Down the hill, down, down. Liam headed for Cole, hoping to catch him before he went inside to Hannah. His breath came quick, but his movements were silent. There were some habits you just couldn't break.

By the time he hit the clearing by the old fire pit, Cole was two feet from opening his front door.

"Hey-" Liam called out, breathless. "Hey, wait."

"Shit!" Cole jumped about two feet and whirled to face him, clapping a hand over his chest. "You sneaky bastard, I didn't hear you coming."

"Yeah..." Liam stopped in front of him and panted a second. "Sorry... I... just... need a... minute."

"For what, Lee?" Cole narrowed his eyes, worried. No one called him Lee. No one except for Cole.

"I need you to recommend me..." Liam stood straighter, having finally caught his breath. "To Hannah. I need you to tell her to give me another chance."

"You want to be with her, too?" Cole huffed a breath at the realization and glanced at the sky briefly. "I thought you hated her."

"Well-" Liam watched his friend struggle, only just now remembering that Cole hadn't wanted to share Hannah to begin with. This may have been a wrong move on Liam's part. This may push Cole just a bit too far. "It was wrong how I acted before, and I've changed. But I understand this is a fucked up situation and I don't want it to come between us. So if you don't want her to see me, then I understand. I can accept that."

"Lee."

"No, just..." Liam shook his head slightly. "Just forget it. Forget I ever said anything."

"Wait, Lee-"

"No, it's all good," Liam assured him. "I'm sorry I brought it up. Night man."

"Yeah." Cole looked into Liam's eyes sadly. "Night man."

CHAPTER TWENTY-SEVEN_
HANNAH

"You hear all that?" Cole asked.

Hannah nodded, she had heard it.

Stepping into the cabin, Cole shut the door quietly behind him. Hannah was curled up in their bed, still fighting the chill in the air. Cookie had started a fire for her when he walked her down, but that wasn't more than half an hour ago. Only now was it spreading out its warmth.

"So, what do you think?" Cole paused, shedding his coat to toss over the nearby chair.

"I'll talk to Liam tomorrow," Hannah assured him.

Of course, that had been the plan all along, but Cole didn't know it. After much debate and discussion, she and Cookie had decided this little plot would be best executed without Cole's input. There was too much riding on it for Cole to lose his temper and say something that would blow everything out of the water. If any of them knew what Hannah and

Cookie were doing, it would completely backfire. The guys had do think Hannah was choosing her lover based purely on her own desire, not because of their influence.

"So, have you narrowed it down, yet?"

Cole was slowly undressing, shedding his shirt and pants to reveal his strong shoulders, flat stomach and toned legs. He was so handsome, Hannah realized, warming at the sight.

"Top three?" He kept guessing as he threw a few more logs on the fire, then slipped into bed beside her. "Top two? Am I getting anywhere here?"

"Nope." Hannah snuggled down beside him. He didn't need to worry about this, she felt like she could handle it.

"You don't have to do this you know," Cole confided quietly, letting his hands intertwine with her own. "You can change your mind, refuse to go through with it."

"Cole." Hannah sighed, but he kept on going.

"I'll take you away," he suggested for the hundredth time. "It won't be like with Andy. I can protect you."

"Shhhh." Hannah placed her finger against his lips to silence him. "No more talking like this."

Cole's eyes held hers in the dimly lit room. They were so filled with questions and concern, with the internal war he was waging. But the path was suddenly so clear to her that Hannah knew it was the only way. Cole would come to understand. He would get used to it. And she would do her best to keep the peace, keep the balance.

His lips moved beneath her finger as he shifted to lay a

slow kiss against the palm of her hand, then another. The gesture melted her. He melted her, but not tonight. She couldn't allow it tonight, so she pulled her hand away and laid her head on his chest.

"Tomorrow morning I'll make my decision," Hannah told him. She listened to Cole hold his breath and it made her want to cry. This was hurting him, but she steeled herself and whispered the next words anyway. "I'll be spending tomorrow night with someone else."

Cole's whole body went rigid then, but he didn't say anything. She listened to his heart pick up the pace. The longer he held his breath, the harder it seemed to thump. Finally, he released the air he was holding, blowing it slowly out of his mouth and up into the dark.

The guilt that swamped Hannah was unexpected. She thought for sure she had logically dealt with the decision at hand and was prepared to move forward. But the hurt she was so clearly causing to the man who lay beside her was overwhelming.

"Who is it?"

"I haven't decided, yet."

"But you're still mine tonight," Cole said, his voice strained.

Shifting to the side, he rolled her onto her back and lowered himself on top of her. Kissing her neck at first, he worked up beneath her chin, to her cheeks and then all over her face. Hannah felt herself responding to his touch, felt herself wanting to give in. But if this was ever going to work, there had to be rules. She couldn't give herself to two men and not set up some boundaries.

"You had me this morning," she reminded him.

As playfully as possible she wriggled out from under him and pressed her palm against his chest. He stilled then, watching her through narrowed eyes. This wasn't the answer he wanted to hear, but she would have to make him listen.

And beyond that, she would have to make him listen without letting him walk out the door. If he didn't buy in, if he didn't agree to this, then there was no point in trying at all. Reaching her hand down, she let her fingers dance across his belly.

"Things are going well for the rescue?" She asked, her hand drifting to his hips, then back up.

"Yeah," he exhaled, his mind was distracted.

"You've come up with a good plan," she commented. "Everyone seems happy with it."

"Uh-huh."

"You're keeping them all together, you're keeping them all safe," she added, her fingers circled his belly button, then began to trace a line steadily down. "They're listening to you again. They respect you."

"Han-" Cole frowned, his head lifting up to look at her.

"I love you, Cole," she said simply, and was rewarded with his expression of utter relief. "But for the days that I am with this other man, then I am *with* him. No public affection, not on either side. I know you won't want to see it. And I can't let you sleep with me the night before I switch, and I won't let him either. Okay?"

Cole swallowed hard once and looked away. For the longest moment, she watched him think, his teeth grinding all the while inside his head. Eventually, he gave a curt nod.

"How long?" His voice was a whisper. "How long will you be... away from me?"

"Two nights."

He nodded again and went to turn away, but then seemed to think better of it. Rolling back over, he wrapped his arms around her body and pulled her in close. She fell asleep with the steady rise and fall of his chest pressed against her back.

<hr />

It was Cookie's voice that woke her in the early hours of the morning. A heavy mist spread outside the solitary window. It was more than just cold out, it was a damp sort of chill. Grumbling beside her in bed, Cole threw his arm across her stomach and glanced to the door.

"What the hell?" He asked, all groggy with sleep.

"Hannah." Cookie ignored him. "Better hurry."

"I'm up," she answered, crawling over Cole and onto the icy floor.

Again Cole groaned, "What the hell?"

"I'll be back, you go to sleep," she told him.

Wrapping her arms around herself, Hannah tried unsuccessfully to keep warm. Her body began to shiver but she took the few short steps to the dresser and changed quickly into a several layers of winter clothes. After shrugging into her heavy fleece-lined jacket, Hannah stacked a few more logs on the still warm coals from last night's fire and turned to the bed.

Cole eyed her but didn't offer any more comments. She leaned forward then, not having intended to do it, and kissed him briefly on the lips. He returned the kiss, sitting up to tangle his hands in her hair before releasing her to go.

Outside, Cookie was nowhere to be seen. The fire pit was cold and empty, the cabins were all dark and silent. It was dawn, with the beginning cast of muted yellow rays just touching at the eastern sky. Hannah shoved both hands deep into the pockets of her jacket and hurried her steps towards the pasture.

They had spent so much time setting this up, she didn't want to be late and miss the whole thing. Liam was slaughtering the lamb today and she had to witness him do it. She just had to.

Cookie said she was out of her mind. He couldn't quite understand her request. But the two of them had narrowed her choices down to Davey and Liam. Though Cookie had given her his opinion, in the end he had agreed that the final decision was hers and hers alone. After all, she was the one who would be lying beside the man night after night.

And that was why Hannah needed to see this so badly. She felt she knew Davey well enough. He was an open book, everyone spoke highly of him. Sure, he'd been a soldier like all the rest of them. He had killed people. But all of the men, by their own admission, had done terrible things during the war. The way they spoke about Liam though, well... he frightened them.

It wasn't the fact that he killed, or even how many. It was the way he did it. The ruthlessness, the cold-blooded pleasure he seemed to derive from it.

But even despite that, the team still respected him. They sought Liam's opinion, even if he was oftentimes reluctant to provide it. If some of the men wanted to leave, then they would all want him to go too. He was a warrior you wanted on your side, no doubt. And if Liam was ever the one to leave... well, he would take more than half of them with him.

Arriving at the pasture fence, Hannah peeked over the top rail and saw Liam sitting in the dewey morning grass. Beside him was the little white lamb.

Cookie had coached her on how to approach him. He had explained what she needed to do if she wanted to see how he killed. And she did want to see. She had to see.

Because at the moment that he took this animal's life, Hannah felt if she could just look into his face, she would get her answers. Did he take pleasure in the act of killing everything? Or was it just "bad" men that turned him so brutal?

Slipping easily through the wooden slots in the gate, Hannah placed her boots slowly and carefully. She controlled her breathing, trying to slow everything down, be as absolutely silent as she could. And it wasn't a foreign concept to her. With Andy, she had learned to disappear into the wilderness, so she used that knowledge now.

As she neared him, she saw that Liam had his arm slung over the lamb's fluffy white back. The animal was munching on something, but they were facing away from her, towards the creek. She thought maybe it was the grass, but as she got within a few yards, she noted the grain bucket from the storeroom. That's when she heard Liam talking.

"It's not fair," he murmured, speaking aloud to himself.

No, Hannah realized after a beat, that wasn't quite right. He wasn't talking to himself... he was talking to the sheep.

"You were supposed to have a whole year, yet."

The animal paused in its crunching, head lifting up for a moment, then ducking back down. Liam stroked the wool along the lamb's back, then patted at his small head.

"In another life," Liam went on quietly. "You could've had a whole herd of lady sheep all to yourself. You'd have been a big ole' bastard with a flock of kids and a shaggy sheep dog to look after you. But we fucked it all up, buddy. We fucked it up good."

Liam's hand stilled, and the sheep nudged him to keep going. For the briefest moment, Hannah thought he would keep petting the animal. But instead, he drew his other hand smoothly beneath the lamb's neck. It was so fast, the lamb didn't even jerk before collapsing forward. Blood poured out onto the grass, and all over Liam's hands.

"Fuck," Liam whispered, his head dropping then just a bit. "I'm sorry."

Staring at the pair of them, Hannah forgot herself. At the sight of the blood, she sucked in a sharp breath.

Whirling at the noise, Liam glanced over his shoulder and locked eyes with her. For a split second, he looked so defeated, so beyond sad. But then he was turning away, swearing and pushing up. Hannah froze on the spot. It was all she could do to keep from shaking.

"Really?!" Liam stood up, his blood soaked hands stretching out at his sides, palms towards her. He'd dropped the knife down in the grass, forgotten. "Now? Why come now? Of all times?"

Hannah didn't answer him. She just watched the raw emotions play across his face. A face that he always kept so carefully masked with anger, disdain or indifference.

For a moment he looked as if he wanted to cry, but then he released a string of curses and stormed a few feet further down the hill. Well, she had her answer, Hannah thought. Reaching into the back pocket of her jeans, she removed her own small knife from its sheath and walked to where the dead animal lay.

While Liam still faced the creek, she crouched down, her back to him. Flipping the lamb over, Hannah began the process of gutting and cleaning it, just the way Andy had shown her. It was dead already, there was no sense wasting the fact.

"What are you doing?" Liam spoke, she could feel him hovering behind her.

Ducking her head, Hannah didn't answer. Truth be told, she didn't trust her voice at the moment. Better just to focus on the work itself, then hopefully her nerves would settle.

Besides, Cookie would be along shortly, wanting to trim off the fat himself to make sure it was clean. If any meat got into the fat, then the soap would be rank and useless. It was a long process, one that would take him all day. She didn't want to keep him waiting.

Another minute passed with her working. All the while she felt Liam's eyes on her. Now that she thought about it, the feeling was a familiar one. Over the past months, she had caught him watching her before.

Not able to stand it any longer, Hannah glanced over her shoulder, meeting the stare of his deep brown eyes. It caused a weird sort of churning in her belly, one that left her feeling strangely short of breath. Unlike in the past, he was the first to look away.

Returning to her work, she felt him approach. He took first one step and then another before he bent down a few inches from her and retrieved his fallen knife. She watched his bloody fingers pluck at the handle, listened to the exhale of his breathing. Why did he linger so?

The tension in the air was palpable. It didn't matter if her eyes were on him or not, she could feel every move he made. Finally, he circled around her and knelt down at the other end of the sheep. In silence, they worked quickly to butcher the meat. They stacked all the pieces on a wooden drag Liam had brought down.

By the time they were done, they were both covered in blood. It was up to their wrists, staining their pants and jackets. Hannah swiped her arm across her forehead, her filthy knife still clutched in her hand, trying to rid herself of the sweat that had formed there.

Looking past Liam's broad shoulders, she saw Cookie approaching. He was through the pasture gate already with the sun filling the bottom of the sky in the distance. That meant she was out of time. And although her decision was as plain now as the new day dawning, she still didn't have the right words to say. Liam left her tongue tied, perpetually it seemed.

Standing up, Hannah crossed to him quickly and knelt down before him. He blinked at her in shock, easing back just a touch in order to get a better look at her face.

He was no psycho killer, she knew that for sure now. He was only a bad man among other bad men, doing what came naturally in order to survive. Before he could say anything to her, she leaned forward and kissed him on the lips.

He didn't kiss her back, he was too surprised, and she didn't really give him time to react. The sparking feeling that now jumped through her body was unexpected. Rising to stand above him, she looked down into his eyes, so full of complete confusion.

"I'll see you tonight," she managed, before walking away.

CHAPTER TWENTY-EIGHT_
COLE

A̶FTER H̶ANNAH HAD LEFT, C̶OLE MUST HAVE FALLEN BACK to sleep because the next thing he knew his front door was banging open and she was already stepping back inside. Lifting his head from the pillow, Cole took one look at her and his heart jumped into his throat. She was covered in blood.

"Han-" Cole shoved back the covers and crossed to her in two steps. "Are you alright? Are you hurt?"

"No." Hannah was breathless as she closed the door behind her.

"Did Liam do this? Did he cut you?"

"No, Cole-"

"Holy shit. You actually stabbed him this time?"

"It was the lamb!" Hannah had to shout at him to make herself heard. Once she had his attention she continued in a quiet voice. "I helped Liam butcher the lamb, that's all."

"Oh." Cole frowned.

Reaching out, he ran his hands down the sleeves of her jacket. There was dried blood all over her coat and pants, staining her hands and smudging along her forehead and right cheek. Her face was flushed, her tangle of golden hair hung down to one side. She looked strained, like whatever had just happened had really affected her. When he went to draw her in closer, she resisted.

"I'd like to clean myself up," she explained, and Cole nodded at that.

The tub that he and Davey had made for her was really quite small. And for the size, it had taken an awful lot of work. They had chopped down the widest tree they could find, estimating they would need about a six foot long section. Davey had figured it would be sort of like making a canoe and in the end it did resemble one, though it was a touch shorter than they would have liked.

Despite days of chipping and smoothing out the inside, there were still some rough patches. It was better than nothing though, and it held water.

Whenever Hannah took a bath, which wasn't too often, Cole liked to sit around and watch. She was so pretty, her skin so smooth and soft. When she was done she'd typically throw on one of his big t-shirts and set about using the leftover water to wash their clothes and blankets.

He liked seeing her wear his clothes. He liked seeing her doing laundry in their tiny home with the cold wind blowing outside. It almost made him forget. Almost.

Then his thoughts would go pinging around, reminding him that the world really had ended. They weren't hiding away in some remote cabin for a weekend vacation. They weren't getting ready to return to the city, one filled with their jobs and their friends. No. All that "normal" was gone.

In its place was this alternate reality. Any day, a group of other men could show up to the compound looking to trade something or take everything. When that happened, he would have to hide Hannah. If any of the others caught sight of her... well, then they would have to die. Dead men don't tell tales and all that.

He didn't want to kill more people but if word ever got out that they had a woman here, then the compound would quickly become overrun. With a shake of his head, Cole rid himself of the worry. He didn't want Hannah to see his concern. He'd protect her. She didn't need the stress.

"I've got three buckets of water inside but they're cold." Cole cleared his throat. "It will take an hour to warm them."

"That's alright."

Hannah moved past him and went to stand in front of the fire. The logs she'd tossed on when she'd left earlier were burning well now. Cole watched her hold her hands out to the warmth, then stare down into the flames.

"Have you decided yet?"

It was the question on everyone's mind, but it had been tormenting Cole in particular. When Hannah remained silent, refusing even to glance over at him, Cole bit back the string of words he wanted to say and instead fetched the buckets of water. Positioning a metal grate over the hottest part of the fire, he set down first one tall wooden bucket and then another beside it. It was a game of waiting and watching, making sure the buckets didn't catch fire and the water inside didn't boil.

"You don't have to do this." Cole tried again, stepping up next to her, reaching his hand out to grab hers. "We can go north, find a spot so remote no one will ever find us. I'll build another cabin, one bigger than this, and-"

"Stop." Hannah squeezed his hand tight, shifting her eyes to plead with his. "I don't want to leave the compound."

"But-"

"Stop, Cole." Hannah pulled her hand away and the gesture sent a new fear to streak through him. He couldn't lose her in all this. "Do you really think we can leave here in winter and survive?"

"Well, I..."

"Are you going to just abandon all the guys on this mission? What about the woman trapped there? I left her once. I can't live with myself if I don't help them find her. I need your support, can't you see it? I need you to help me do this, please."

"You can change your mind. You can just say no." Cole grabbed for her again, but she stepped away.

"And what would all the guys think then?" Hannah's eyes darted over his face. "How could they trust you to lead, or trust me for anything? They'd think we just played them."

"I don't..." Cole squeezed his eyes shut, his head tipping back to the ceiling. "Know. I don't know."

"Maybe I should just go wash at Liam's place," Hannah mumbled the words in a rush. "I can't argue with you anymore."

Cole's stomach dropped as his head snapped back into place. A wave of panic kicked up the flow of blood through his body as his buddy's name repeated itself over in his mind.

Liam's place. Liam. She had chosen his best friend and suddenly she could walk out his door and never look back if she wanted.

"No." Cole gave his head a quick shake. "You don't need to leave."

He stepped back slowly until he could feel the front door behind him. With a sharp intake of breath, he leaned his body against it. He could *not* let her go. The idea of her walking out that door and into Liam's cabin made him want to throw up, then beat the shit out of something, then throw up again. He tried to hide it, tried to control his reaction, but Hannah must have seen right through him because she gave him a sad sort of smile.

"I'll never leave you." Hannah kept those doe eyes fixed on his. "This is all *for* you."

"He's my best friend," Cole sputtered. "I've known him all my life, like since we were five."

"I didn't know that."

"Why him?" Cole's voice cracked just a touch, betraying him.

Liam was the one person Cole turned to for solid advice. He was his secret keeper, his backup. For as long as Cole could remember Liam had been there, supporting him, fighting alongside him. He was more than a friend, he was a brother... he was *family*. The only family Cole had left.

Hannah remained silent, but as she crossed to Cole, she never let her eyes move from his.

"Why him, Han?" Cole repeated himself, then added. "I *need* him."

Then it dawned on him clear as day and his eyes grew wide with the realization. That was why she chose Liam, because Cole needed him.

"You're going to rescue this woman." Hannah reached out and took Cole's bunched up fist into her own hands. "If she's still alive, then there will be two of us and hopefully still eight of you. That doesn't take care of everyone, it doesn't even come close.

But what if we could show the team that this sharing thing could work? With a lot of time and patience... what if you and Liam and I set the example? Maybe this woman would be willing to try it too, eventually. Maybe we could keep the team together, keep the compound, stay safe and alive."

"Just me and Liam, right?" Cole's gut tripped sickeningly. "No one else?"

"Right."

"I still don't know. I already want to kick his face in."

"We have to treat this for what it is." Hannah used her

fingers to slowly, gently open Cole's hand. "An alliance between friends. We're going to have to really try to make it work. It's not going to be easy. But we can do this, *if* we make sure to respect each other."

Cole swallowed hard. He wanted to die. He wanted to beat the shit out of Liam then let himself fucking explode. *But your buddy didn't do anything wrong.* The pestering nagging voice inside him piped up. *Can you blame him for wanting to be with a woman after so many years?*

Blinking hard, Cole let his eyes find Hannah. She was so close to him now, touching him and watching him. His heart tripped. *You're in love with this woman. You have to protect her. Have to keep her alive. Can you really do that all alone? Or will she end up just like she says, in some bastard's steel cage with you lying dead on the ground?*

"And you still love me." Cole held his breath, the feel of her hands on his made him ache.

"And I still love you." Hannah stood up on her tip toes and brought her face close to his before pressing a soft kiss to his mouth.

It undid him. She undid him, everytime.

CHAPTER TWENTY-NINE_
LIAM

THE CREEK WASN'T *LIKE* BATHING IN ICE, IT *WAS* BATHING IN ice. But Liam was filthy and there was no easy way around it. So he stood there up to his waist in water, naked, shaking like a damn leaf in the wind. He always brought a bar of soap and a change of clothes with him when he slaughtered. But this far into fall, it was rare that he would venture all the way into the stream.

Cookie crouched on the nearby bank, trimming his precious fat and running his mouth the way he always did.

"Never have seen you this gung-ho for keeping clean," Cookie cackled. "Must a been that kiss that did it."

"You talk too damn much, old man." Liam's teeth chattered as he said the words. One more dunk and he should be properly washed.

"She chose you then, huh?"

"I don't know," Liam admitted, though he could still feel her kiss on his lips.

Cookie huffed a breath that had Liam glancing at him over his shoulder. If he didn't know better, he could have sworn the old man was smiling. Sucking in a breath, Liam counted to three before plunging all the way under the steady flow of water. His heart screamed at him and his skin tightened in pain, but then he was shoving back up to break the surface and dashing out onto the bank.

Panting, he stepped quickly into his fresh clothes, not having bothered to bring a towel with him. Cold. Too cold. He had to think of a better way to do that. Especially if what Cookie was saying was true, if that kiss wasn't his last and Hannah was going to give him another chance.

"She said she'd talk to me again tonight," Liam offered, which was unusual for him. He didn't like to give information out the way the others so readily did.

"That's not what I heard."

Liam waited for the older man to continue but Cookie just kept at his work. Running out of patience, Liam turned to trudge up the hill alone. He had better things to do than play this sort of cat and mouse game all damn day. Besides, Cookie sure was taking his sweet time trimming, and the lamb had been so small he wouldn't need help hauling the meat up the hill.

But then Liam just couldn't help himself. Despite his desire to leave, impulse and maybe a touch of desperation had him staying.

"What did you hear?" Liam let his words leak out between clenched teeth, knowing he was playing right into Cookie's hands.

"I believe she said: *I'll see you tonight.*"

"Same difference."

"Not really."

"What do you know about it?" Liam cried finally, gripping his hands in his hair. Would the asshole just spell it out already? "What are you trying to say?"

"She never kissed any of us. Never gave out no second interview, either." Cookie ignored the direct question, as usual, opting instead for his own brand of explanation.

Liam growled in frustration before giving up altogether and hiking for the fence line. The damn old coot with his half words and hidden meanings, it grated on Liam's last nerve. That's all he needed, Liam thought, false hope.

But try as he might to talk himself down, the feel of Hannah's mouth against his had set sparks flying all inside of him. He wanted her now more than he ever had. Which would make things all that much worse if he made a fool of himself by declaring something that maybe wasn't one-hundred percent... yet.

So Liam moved through the pasture gate, clutching his bloody clothes in one hand, and headed for his cabin. The sun had moved itself higher in the sky now, and if keeping time would still have been a thing, Liam would have judged it to be about nine in the morning. Breakfast was going to be late, Cookie was busy and no one that Liam knew of had been assigned the task.

On the one hand, he couldn't stand the idea of eating right now. His nerves were pumping and the uncertainty that still hung over him left him slightly sick. But on the other, Liam felt suddenly ravenous, like he could consume a whole plate of scrambled eggs with cheese and hot sauce.

God how he missed eggs and cheese and hot sauce. They had no chickens and though the goat produced some milk, it wasn't very much. The guys took turns drinking it but there was barely any cream left over to make butter. They didn't have the right stuff to even try cheese. You needed vinegar or lemon juice to make it separate, or so said Cookie, the almighty authority on all things food related.

Arriving at his home, Liam dropped the clothes at his doorstep and entered his work shed instead. There, lying in the low light of the room, the bracelet sparkled at him. Had she really just chosen him? Had Hannah actually just picked Liam, without ever receiving her jewelry or listening to him apologize?

The thought bloomed, then threatened to quickly overtake him. Was she actually going to be his tonight? Cole must have put in a good word for him after all, Liam realized. He owed him. He owed him so, so big.

CHAPTER THIRTY_
HANNAH

THE STONE HOUSE WAS WARM. FLAMES ROARED IN THE fireplace and off to one side, Hannah fried breaded lamb cutlets on a flat iron griddle. It was dinnertime, and the guys had slowly but surely filtered in to fill the space.

Cookie had been busy most of the day making soap so she'd offered to prepare the evening meal. Using a bit of milk from the goat, Hannah coated the raw cutlets before covering them in the ground corn-flour.

Mostly, the group's meat was cut into small pieces and used in soups, chili and stews. It made for a larger quantity of hot food for the guys and the protein had a way of seeping into the broth. So it was a rare treat for them to get individual pieces of meat like this, especially ones so fresh. The vast majority of their food was cured, smoked or dried to make it last longer.

"Man that smells amazing." Ryder had crept up beside her, sniffing greedily at the smokey air.

"Thank you." Hannah turned to give him a smile and he actually blushed.

He was so sweet, really. It was a shame that she could never have chosen him. Maybe the woman that they rescued would eventually be interested in him. That hope alone seemed to have raised everyone's spirits.

Hannah had expected some mixed responses from the guys once they figured out who she had picked, but to her surprise they all seemed real okay with it. Maybe it was the impending rescue mission, the hope for the other woman or maybe even more than one. Whatever it was that kept the mood playful, Hannah appreciated it very much.

And word had obviously gotten out that Liam was the one because the moment he walked in the door, the guys began to tease him mercilessly. Glancing over her shoulder at him, Hannah watched his eyes track to her and hold. He didn't come over to her or say anything, and she hadn't expected him to. There was something so reserved, so careful about Liam. He never left himself hanging out for anyone to really see.

Shifting back to her work, Hannah stirred the giant pot of boiling potatoes and stabbed a bunch of pickled carrots out of a large jar. She would heat them up in the grease left over by the lamb.

Her day had been spent inside, mostly in an attempt to avoid everyone. She didn't come to lunch, but instead had Cole bring it to her inside his cabin. Though she told him it was because she needed to finish their wash, she was sure he knew the real reason. Hannah hadn't been quite ready to see them all. She needed time to put her brave girl face on.

But for the most part, her fears had been unwarranted. Everyone still joked and talked to her and no one looked properly pissed that she had gone with someone else. It was a nice feeling to be accepted by them in this way. She would try to remember it, in case it all went to hell in the end.

"Alright, guys," Hannah called, dusting her hands off as she stepped back. "Come fill your plates."

There was a rumble of appreciation and the sound of shifting chairs and shuffling boots. One by one they came to pass by the fire, filling their empty dishes with the meal she had prepared. Cookie was the first in line and he scrutinized the food with care. To Hannah's amazement, he had nothing bad to say. She reached out to run her hand down his arm, and he rewarded her with a sly wink before moving on.

Then came Davey with Ryder just behind. Standing so close together, the family resemblance was undeniable.

"Any chance I can get a consolation prize?" Davey teased, and had the others hooting. "Maybe a kiss on the cheek?"

Hannah laughed then and glanced around. Cole hadn't come in yet, he was the last one. Normally she would have looked to him for a cue, but left to her own devices she simply nodded and smiled.

Leaning forward, she gave Davey a peck on the cheek. The crowd cheered and Ryder stepped up next, turning his face and waiting. How could she resist? It was all in good fun. So Hannah kissed him on the cheek too, then Ace, then Trey. Each of them tried to outdo the one before, saying something funny or making a silly face.

When Liam stepped up to fill his plate, the guys grew quiet and everyone watched what she would do. Hannah had to look decidedly up at him, he was so very much taller than she. Her tummy fluttered a bit and she couldn't quite keep the hint of a blush from creeping up her neck and into her cheeks. Why was she reacting this way? She didn't know and felt suddenly guilty and unsure.

Liam bent down so that his face was level with hers and ducked his head once before giving her the smallest of kisses on the cheek. The guys groaned and complained loudly, but they all had smiles spreading across their faces. Hannah's eyes flicked up to Liam's and she had never felt so grateful to him. How did he know just what to do to make it okay?

He smiled then, a private one just for her, before stepping away and taking a seat at the table. After the rest had all sat down, Hannah filled her own plate and wondered where Cole was. Just as the feeling of worry began to spread, the door to the stone house was shoved open and he walked inside.

The room dropped into silence. It was the first time that Cole and Liam had been in the same space since she made her choice. The tension was palpable.

"Boy-o!" Cookie called. "You're late."

"Yeah," Cole acknowledged, his eyes sought Hannah first, then moved to Liam.

For a split second the old friends eyed one another and Hannah's pulse began to race. But then Liam was standing and skirting the table. He held out his hand for Cole to shake and after a moment's hesitation, Cole took it.

"Don't make me kick your ass," Cole grumbled.

"I won't." Liam threw Hannah a look over his shoulder before returning his eyes to his friend. "I promise."

"Maybe you two lovers should have a go first, huh?!" Ace quipped.

Laughter rippled through the room as Liam returned to his seat and some of the others made raunchy comments of their own. Hannah exhaled slowly before handing her plate to Cole who took his seat at the head of the table.

With her back to all of them, they couldn't see how her hands shook as she made up one more plate for herself.

This could work.

This was going to work.

This had to work... didn't it?

The meal itself went smoothly enough. Hannah sat in her usual seat next to Cole, though she thought probably she should have sat beside Liam since she would be staying with him tonight. The habits and rules that would guide this situation weren't all the way formed yet. Hannah was having to work on the fly, making things up as she went along.

Conversation was easy and focused mainly on the

rescue which would start, come snow or shine, in three days time. Trey and Cookie had been selected to stay behind and guard the compound while the others went off to play hero. The one point that was still heavily up for debate was the use of the mule and cart. It would slow them down considerably but could be used to carry supplies, weapons, additional ammo and hay for the horses.

They also didn't know what condition the woman was in. Maybe she wouldn't be able to walk, or even ride a horse. The more they hashed things out, the more clear it became that they would need to bring it along and sacrifice their stealth for practicality.

Liam and Cole were the best riders, and the horses pretty much "belonged" to them, although they could technically be used by any member of the team. Hannah watched quietly as Cole accepted advice, listened to concerns and made no outright decisions. Once the meal had been consumed, he rose from the table and began to subtly work the room. She had seen him do it before.

He sat with Ace and convinced him to bring less ammo, then he moved to Ryder and offered him a shift on horseback. It was impressive and... Hannah searched in her mind for the right word. *Political*, she thought, it was very political of him. Odd, she wasn't quite sure of the implication.

Rising to her feet, Hannah began to clear dishes when she heard Cookie call out to her.

"Pretty sure it's Ace's turn," he said, causing the other man to groan.

Hannah ducked her head in acceptance and set her plate back down but remained standing. It was time to get out of here.

Eyes jumping to Liam, she noted he was still seated at the table but his plate was pushed back and empty now. Chan was talking to him intently about something, gesturing every once in awhile, his hands moving quickly through the air. Liam was nodding, but as usual, wasn't saying much.

It was rare that she had the chance to observe him this way and it only lasted a second. He must've felt her looking at him because his dark eyes shot up to hers and it made her whole body tense. Heat filled her cheeks once more and she felt embarrassed, like she had been caught doing something she shouldn't.

Fingers tightening against the edge of the table, Hannah let her eyes drop and she turned away towards the door. It was hard to tell whether the room felt silent because it actually was, or because the sound of her beating heart was so loud it was the only thing she could hear.

Right before she shoved out into the darkness, Hannah chanced a glance behind her. Cole was in the corner with his back to her, speaking to a group of the guys. Liam hadn't moved from his spot. His dark eyes continued to shine at her, as if they could see through her and into her all at once.

With a quick intake of breath, she left them both there and stepped greedily into the cold night air. The swirling wind hit her face, whipping her hair behind her as she turned into it, welcomed it. Liam's cabin was just down the hillside through the thick trunks of pine and maple and oak.

She had only been inside the one time before, when she had returned his laundry. That day seemed so long ago, now. It was the first time he had acknowledged her without a frown filling his face and she had known then that the group was beginning to accept her.

Liam had always been standoffish. From the very first, she knew he disapproved of Cole's decision to let her stay. But after awhile she felt she was making progress with him. He was letting down his defenses and if he didn't like her very much then at least he appeared neutral.

That's why it came as such a surprise when she overheard him ask Cole to recommend him to her. Up until that point, both Cookie and she weren't certain Liam would even be willing to have her. And he was clearly a pivotal member of the team. So though he made her nervous at times, Hannah knew Liam was the one she should really be targeting. If she could keep him *and* Cole, then the others would stay.

Glancing over her shoulder, Hannah half expected to see Liam leave the stone house and come following behind her, but he wasn't there. A part of her felt disappointment at the realization and then she shook her head and wondered at herself. Liam had always brought out some strange mix of emotions she couldn't quite name.

Ahead of her, his cabin appeared in the woods and she slowed her pace as the hillside dropped sharply just above it. Skirting down around one side, she noted the one window he had was closed up tight but a faint glow emanated from it. Must be from the fire, she thought, walking around to the front door before coming to a stop.

Her hand reached out and clutched the leather strap that served as a sort of door handle. It was worn and she let her thumb play over it as she considered what she was about to do. Maybe she should have asked, or talked to him before she just assumed she was welcome inside.

Dropping her hand, Hannah took a step back, then frowned at herself. An icy push of wind cut sharply across her face. It was silly to stand here in the weather, waiting for Liam to show up. He had asked to be considered by her and this is what he got. Straightening her shoulders, she pulled on the strap and opened the heavy door. When she saw what was inside, her mouth dropped in shock.

There was a lamp sitting on a table. The tiny source of its light was magnified by its glass globe, throwing the room into a sort of warm glow. His wide mattress was up off the floor, positioned on a wooden bed frame in the far corner.

Swiveling her head to the left she spied a chair pushed into the other corner with a series of low shelves hung along the length of one wall. His clothes were all neatly stacked on them. This was nothing like the dusty empty place she remembered.

A fire burned hot in his forge, making the room so

warm she felt the need to remove her jacket. Forgetting that the door was open wide behind her, Hannah shed her outer layer and unlaced her boots. She noted the floor was swept clean now and she didn't want to track in mud.

Stepping out of her shoes she padded in her socks over to the table with the lamp. It had a series of drawers attached under one side. There was a special name for it when it had drawers like this. It was a... a... *desk*, she thought, and actually smiled to herself.

That's when the glint of metal caught her eye. It was a shining silver thing winking at her from the surface of the desk. Inching ever closer, she reached out and picked it up. It was beautiful. Holding it up in the light she marveled at the tiny flowers carved into each metal link.

"Do you like it?" Liam's low voice came from just behind her, causing her to jump visibly.

"Oh!" Hannah exclaimed, dropping it back down to the tabletop. "I'm sorry, I should have asked-"

"No." Liam shook his head and turned away to shut the door. "I made it for you."

When he turned back around to face her, Hannah suddenly realized how alone they were. She was here in his cabin, standing a few feet from him. The door was shut. Suddenly, her heart began tripping about in her chest, as if searching for something to hold onto. They hadn't hardly shared more than a few sentences in all their time together.

Liam tilted his head to one side, watching her. After a beat he sucked in a breath and ducked his head, skirting around to feed another log to the fire. Hannah leaned back against the desk and kept her eyes on his broad back. He adjusted the air vent on the forge, kicked off his boots and placed them next to hers by the door, then shed his jacket and hung it on an empty hook.

All the while, he kept his eyes from meeting hers. It was as if he was giving her some space to settle. Looking down at the desk once more, Hannah spied the metal circle and reached for it. He made this for her. That's what he'd said.

"When?" She asked. Then cleared her throat when he looked at her, eyebrows raised in question. "I mean, when did you make this... for me."

"The bracelet?"

"Bracelet," she repeated and glanced down to her wrist. *Yes, that's where it goes.*

"Well it took me a long time." Liam's eyes bounced from her face to her wrist and back. "I started it over a month ago."

Hannah frowned, thinking about the timeline as Liam approached her. Reaching out, he lowered one large hand to cover hers, his thumb smoothing gently over the skin on the inside of her wrist. Her breath hitched and her body tingled.

"Can I put it on you?" He asked.

Hannah nodded, noting the way the tingles traveled up her arm from the place he touched, then down to her belly and lower. Taking the bracelet from her, he looped it around her right wrist. It felt cool and smooth against her skin. She ran the fingers of her left hand over it, admiring the detail in his work.

"Liam," Hannah began, her eyes flicking up to lock with his. "If you started this that long ago, then it was when-"

"When you were only going to be with Cole?" Liam supplied, and then gave her such a look of intensity, she lost her words. "You really have no idea what you do to me... do you?"

He took a step closer and when she tried to retreat she bumped into the desk and stopped. Reaching behind her, he put out the lamp so that the light in the cabin appeared dusky and low. The movement brought their bodies even closer together. She could feel the heat radiating from him, inhaled the mix of fresh soap and rough man that permeated the air.

He was so much bigger than she was. Taller, with defined shoulders and a chiseled jaw. She tilted her chin up to look at his face. He was handsome, very much so. How had she not noticed it before?

Flickering flames from the fire danced around causing shadows to move over the walls. Hannah drew in a sharp breath and held it. The swirling butterflies that had suddenly appeared inside her wanted to get out.

"Can I show you?" He whispered the question, his eyes roaming over her face. "Will you let me show you what you do to me?"

Looking first into his dark eyes, Hannah let her gaze drop to his strong jaw and smooth chin. He never let a beard grow there, not the way Cole did.

Lifting her hand, Hannah hesitated only a moment before reaching up to stroke at the skin of his cheek. She never did give him a verbal answer, but that gesture seemed to be the only encouragement he needed.

Slowly, he began unbuttoning the front of her shirt. Well, again it was Cole's shirt really. One she had cut down to her size. Swallowing, Hannah pushed thoughts of Cole from her mind and gripped the edge of the desk behind her.

Liam took his time, letting his eyes travel along the opening in her shirt until he was able to push it off her shoulders. It slipped back to crumple in a heap on the desk. That's when he kissed her. Lowering his mouth to hers once, twice, backing away each time to glance into her eyes.

He was testing, lingering, letting his lips travel down her neck, to her collar bone and back up beneath her chin. All the while he kept his hands feather light, gliding over her hips, around to her lower back, up the length of her spine. She shivered and her breath caught just a bit in her throat. When she looked into his eyes, he let a knowing smile spread across his face.

"You're the most beautiful woman that I've ever seen," he murmured.

Then his arms circled around her waist and he drew her up against him, pressing her bare chest against the soft cotton of his shirt. Laying his mouth on hers, he kissed her deeper this time, parting her lips, dipping his tongue inside. She felt herself kiss him back, she couldn't help it.

Originally, she had wanted this to be more like a business transaction. Or maybe how it had been with Andy, short and to the point. But before she knew what was happening Liam had lifted her off her feet and in a few short steps had laid her out on his bed, still kissing her all the while.

A heat spread from her core out and it rippled pleasantly inside of her. Her heart hammered. Her belly clutched. When he loosened the snap of her jeans she arched her body up, helping him to pull them down around her hips, to her legs, and away.

Reaching out for him, Hannah's hands found his shirt and lifted it above his head. She wanted to feel his ripple of taut muscles beneath her palms. He was strong, really strong.

Crawling over her, Liam lowered his mouth to hers, kissing her deeply for several seconds before pulling away. Then his mouth was tracing down the length of her body. Slowly, from her cheeks and chin to her breasts and stomach, over her hips and down the length of her thighs. He didn't stop there but continued to kiss down to the tips of her toes before taking her feet in his hands and rubbing them.

Hannah tilted her head up to watch. Her body ached for more of what he was doing. More of his hands on her. More. His eyes traveled over her as his hands glided back up to her hips. Gently, his fingers pulsed along her sides before he flipped her over to lay her on her stomach.

Nervous jitters cruised through her body and she turned her face to the side to look back at him. He gave her a slight smile as he bent to lay a kiss on her shoulder. Then his hands shifted up to rub her back.

Everywhere he touched, his lips followed. Everything he did was drawn out, causing a sort of relaxed wanting to build inside her. She felt damp and hot and needy. As he glanced up from his rubbing the look on his face told her he knew it. He knew exactly what he was doing to her.

Then his hands were back on her hips, lifting them up in the air, urging her to make space for him. Laying on his back, Liam slid his face between her legs. The moment his mouth found her center, she gasped, hands clenching the fabric of the blankets.

Pleasure flooded her, flowing out from where he licked and sucked and kissed until she heard herself whimpering and moaning in turn. At any moment, she thought he would stop, but he just kept on going. He kept going until she buried her face in the blankets and cried out, clenching tightly around nothing. The release he brought to her was blinding.

Turning her face to the side once more, she lay still, panting and slightly stunned.

Without a word Liam slipped out from beneath her. She listened to him taking off his pants. Then he lowered himself down on top of her, laying his chest against her back. His breath exhaled over her neck and he pushed her hair to one side. Smoothing his other hand over her butt, his fingertips traced around her hips until he found her front and began circling her there.

Tensing, her body jumped a bit beneath him. The touch

was almost too much so soon after. But as he worked his fingers, she felt his hips pressing up behind her. Before she had time to think, he was guiding himself inside of her and she let out a gasping groan. It felt good. He felt good.

As he rocked against her, sliding in and out, she felt him lay his forehead against the skin of her back. He kissed along her spine, then up between her shoulder blades before biting back a groan of his own. The sound of him sent a fresh rush of pleasure through her.

Tilting her hips, she pushed back against him until his pace quickened reflexively. Somehow he managed to keep his one hand steady as he stroked her, even though his breath was coming out harsh and broken.

All of a sudden she felt incredibly hot, like her body was on fire. The intensity she felt was gaining, coming on more and more with each thrust he made. She could feel him everywhere, moving inside her, over her, around her.

Squeezing her eyes shut, she gasped as he nipped at her shoulder, his teeth gently scraping her skin. Then she was coming, so fast that she cried out, pulsing and clenching all around him.

He cursed under his breath and came at her harder. She gasped. With her belly pressed down into the mattress, she listened to him moaning into her hair. Felt his release fill her, his body surround her.

For several minutes after, they lay still like that, him on top of her, still inside her. Hannah had to work to catch her breath. She felt dizzy and silly and filled with a lingering ache.

"What…" Hannah panted, lifting her head in an attempt to see him behind her. "Was that?"

Liam let go a light laugh, then a satisfied smile filled his face as he lay his lips once more on her back.

"That… is how you make me feel."

CHAPTER THIRTY-ONE_
COLE

FLAMES WERE LICKING UP THE HALLWAY AS THEY RAN. COLE could feel the heat pulsing all around him. Sweat rolled down his body beneath his blacked out fatigues but he was sure they'd been soaked through already. The time spent facing down his failed executioner is what had done it.

Chan was just ahead of him, the rifle he still held was poised and ready, pointing at the stairwell at the end of the hall. It was unnecessary though, there were no more live men inside the building. Just the two of them, and it should have been just the one.

"Man down, man down!" The screaming inside his headset would not stop. "Taking fire, multiple sources."

"Cook!" Cole barked into his mic. "Where the fuck is our cover?!"

Static crackled in his headset, but he couldn't make out the reply. They passed door upon door left wide open. Glancing briefly inside, Cole saw computers, television screens, towering *tall servers with blinking little lights. And code, their Command Code, running like ticker tape all over the monitors. What the fuck?*

Cole didn't have time to process it. He skidded to a stop just behind Chan who had come to the door and was waiting for Cole's go ahead.

"Drones! Drones! Drones!" Liam's voice echoed in their ears. "Take out the flying fucking saucers!"

With a curt nod, Cole breached the door and they were descending the metal steps. The hollow sound of their running pounded in his ears, making it impossible to hear the exchange of words that still flowed from their headsets.

After two flights they hit bottom. The roll of smoke all around them was sickeningly thick. They coughed and heaved as they flew out that final exit door and onto the unforgiving concrete outside.

Sitting upright in bed, Cole sputtered and coughed. That Godforsaken nightmare of a memory had come back now that Hannah wasn't beside him. He always woke up after that last part. It just felt so real that his body struggled and gasped for fresh air.

The after effects were especially hard to shake during the cold winter months when his makeshift fireplace puffed out smoke all night long. The scent stuck in his nostrils, lined his mouth and made his eyes burn.

This was the second night she'd been gone and it was pure and utter torture. Normally he would have talked to

Liam about something like this, but for obvious reasons that was no longer an option. Their whole arrangement was so fucked. It was like he had been robbed of Hannah and his best friend all in one fell swoop.

Shoving back the covers, Cole paced the short length of his dark cabin. The storm that had been looming was stuck on the mountain range off to the west. He had been planning on leaving in one more day but everything was ready to go and it seemed stupid to wait any longer.

The compound was properly stocked so that Cookie and Trey could defend it easily enough while the rest of them were away. And besides, the team was getting antsy. Hell, he was getting antsy. They needed to get on the move.

Sitting back on the edge of his bed, Cole buried his face in his hands and exhaled a breath. Who was he kidding? There was no going back to sleep now. Crossing to his dresser, Cole layered up then stepped into his boots and shrugged into his heavy coat. Pausing for just a moment, he ran his hand over one of Hannah's shirts before purposefully shoving her from his mind and striding out the door.

Dawn wouldn't come for another hour or more yet, but that didn't mean Cole couldn't get to work. He headed for the pasture, his long strides helped to bring warmth to his body where he only felt empty and cold.

That last mission, that damn failure of a last mission, it made him worry even more about this one. When Cole had made the decision to defect, the others hadn't hesitated to follow. They had ditched the scanner and headsets, anything electronic. Something had been off for awhile, but that last ambush, with their code plastered everywhere inside the building, it was like their own Command had been the one trying to kill them.

Pushing through the pasture gate, Cole could just make out the figures of the livestock grazing down by the creek. The grass was getting pretty sparse and in preparation for what lay ahead, he had begun supplementing them with hay. Where had the hay come from? The seeds and the tools to work the ground and the buckets and the livestock and all of it?

Cole exhaled a breath, watching the steam puff in front of his face briefly before lifting into the air and dissipating. He didn't like to think of the men, who were not soldiers, who lay dead and buried at a farmhouse just a few days hike from this very spot.

So, Cole handled it the way he had countless other things that made him hate himself. He pushed the images from his mind and angled his steps up into the trees.

At the crest of the hill, the mountain provided a clearing with a gently rolling meadow. That was where the team planted, hauled water and tended their crops during the growing season. Right this minute though, it was empty, save for three enormous stacks of loose hay that lay carefully protected under heavy tarps and surrounded by stout fencing.

It would have been difficult to see in the darkness that still clung to the earth, but Cole knew the way there like the back of his hand. His feet had traveled the path countless times. So all he needed was the vague outline, and he had that, with the moon waning and the sun just hinting at its arrival.

Hopping the fence easily, he picked up a large sack from under the edge of the tarp and began filling it with hay. He would haul this back over to the pasture gate and feed the horses there. That way he would be able to grab their halters and tie them to a post. When it was time to go, there wouldn't be any issues.

Of course, that meant he would have to haul water too, or walk them to the creek before they left. But at this point he welcomed the extra work. It helped him not to think. It helped him not to miss Hannah. It helped him not to hate his friend.

CHAPTER THIRTY-TWO_
LIAM

SITTING ASTRIDE HIS BAY HORSE, LIAM FELT THE PUSH OF wind whipping past him to sweep back down the hill. He was high up in the tree line, with the others moving below him, picking their way through the narrow valley that would lead them north. His eyes tracked the rough country that lay ahead. There was an easier way, but it would bring them too close to the territory held by certain other groups of men and Liam wanted to avoid them if at all possible.

Glancing down at the crew, he scrutinized each figure with care. If he hadn't known exactly what to look for, he would've been unable to separate Hannah from the others. They had bound her hair up and tucked it into a ball cap. That combined with the heavy winter jacket and two pairs of pants, she could have been a teenage boy, or a slightly built man.

Even from this distance, the sight of her had his blood

heating. He gave his head a shake, trying to rid himself of the weakness she brought on.

Two nights hadn't been enough, and seeing her return to Cole had been more challenging than Liam had expected. But thankfully she'd made it clear she wouldn't be sleeping with either of them during this trip. They would be in too close of quarters and their little arrangement, as she liked to call it, had to be based off of mutual respect.

Hah, Liam thought, he had forgotten what it was like to be around a woman. So careful and considerate of feelings, not wanting to give the wrong impression.

But deep down he knew it was good that Hannah was running things. Without her, Liam expected that Cole and he would just beat the shit out of each other and whoever was left standing would keep her and that would be that. Without Hannah's delicate planning and unending rules, this sharing thing would not be able to last.

And that was the strangest thing about it... Liam really did want it to last. He did not want to lose Cole, but after that first time with Hannah, he knew he could never give her up either, not for anything.

"Keeping up?" Liam called over his shoulder, and waited for Ryder to appear.

"Yeah."

The kid squeezed the gray horse into a trot and closed the gap between them. Liam spared him a quick frown before pointing to the expanse before them.

"See that copse of trees?" Liam gestured. "The darker ones on the far side of the clearing?"

"Yeah." Ryder leaned forward in the saddle, eager to drink everything in.

"That's what we're aiming for to make camp tonight. It provides cover, and there looks to be a little cut of water that passes just on the west side."

"Good, yeah, water," Ryder agreed, then continued. "Why are we heading north? Didn't Hannah follow us up from the south?"

Liam's eyebrows shot up with surprise and he gave Ryder an appreciative smile. He hadn't known the kid was paying that much attention.

"She did," Liam acknowledged. "But after I interviewed her, I figured she originally came from the north but skirted our mountain to the east then picked up our trail on the south end."

"Alright." Ryder bobbed his head and went to move forward but Liam held up a hand.

"What else do you notice from up here?"

"Notice?"

"Yeah kid, you want to learn, right? Look, tell me what you see."

"Um." Ryder paused and gave the land his full attention. "The crew moving, there's five of them. And just over the rise, there's a doe, no, make that two."

"And?"

"And..." Ryder lifted his gaze further until his eyes tracked the opposing mountain range. "And smoke."

"Good." Liam bobbed his head. "What does that mean?"

"No fire for us tonight." Ryder sighed. "And double the watch."

"Perfect."

Leaning forward ever so slightly in his saddle, Liam signaled his horse to move back down the hill and re-join the team.

They reached the copse of thick trees just after dark. Travel had been slower than expected. They had to stop and double back at one point because the mule couldn't haul the cart up and over a section of large rocks. Still, the spot was a pretty good one. The cut in the land was indeed water, and it flowed clean from the taste of it.

Liam stood beside his horse, letting him drink, his nostrils flaring, his lips sucking greedily at the stream. Cole was beside him, letting his gray do the same.

"I think we need to go over it again," Cole was saying.

"I already told you everything." Liam sighed, but he knew this was coming.

"I want to hear it from her," Cole insisted.

He was talking about the location of the tiny concrete building. The one Hannah had seen with the woman just beside it. Liam had already spent hours reviewing everything with her, but that had been days ago, when they were holed up together in his cabin. Killing time, he thought, time until he could get her under him again. And he had, several times.

A slight smile wanted to tug at the corner of his mouth, but Liam suppressed it. Instead, he threw a look over his shoulder and squinted through the blackness in an attempt to see Hannah.

She was there, moving amongst the others, rolling out all of their sleeping bags beneath the protection of the cart. Without a fire, it was the best way to keep warm. They would all line up side by side, using body heat and the cover of a tarp pulled tight over the wagon and spiked into the ground on four sides.

"Sure thing, Cole," Liam relented, keeping his face straight and plain. "Whatever you need."

Cole nodded at that and the tension that now seemed to plague them eased up a bit. Together, they walked their horses into the thicket, removed their tack and tied them off to a line strung up between two trees. After tossing a few armfuls of hay at their feet, they left them to munch quietly beside the mule.

Back at the cart, everyone was underneath it already, eating. You had to lay down on your belly, or sit hunched under the far edge, but it was already several degrees warmer than outside. By the look of things, they were going to end up tangled in that stalled out storm, the one still dumping loads of snow to their west. Liam wasn't sure about the odds, but figured he could still find the building, eventually.

"Han," Cole addressed her, making Liam flinch just a bit

at the nickname. "I'd like to go over the location of this place again, so that we're all on the same page. Alright?"

"Alright," Hannah echoed him, her voice sounded tired.

She was already tucked down in her sleeping bag, the one that Cookie had lent her for the journey. In his head, Liam had counted out the nights and knew that if they were back at the compound, she would belong to him again. But they weren't, so she had her own bedroll; although it was wedged down between him and Cole.

Equal in public, that's what she'd said. They shouldn't touch or show affection, but if she had to choose who to sit by or who to follow, then she would do her best to make it equal. Liam had fought his desire to roll his eyes or say something rude, reminding himself that nothing was free, least of all the best things. If this was the price he had to pay to be with Hannah, then he would pay it... gladly.

"What's the first thing you remember about that place?" Liam asked. He knew the answer but this was to benefit the others, not him.

"Apart from the crying? It was low." Hannah's voice seemed to intensify at the memory. "I was looking down on it."

"Were you thirsty?"

"No. There was a pond with a little stream that flowed into it. I had drunk from it that morning."

"Did you walk all day?"

"No." Hannah paused. "I slept most of that day, I just started walking at dusk. I think it was an hour before I heard her."

And they went on that way. Liam asking leading questions and Hannah answering. Though Liam couldn't see his friend's face, he knew Cole was absorbing the details, filing them away in his mind, visualizing the location.

They had been taught many things by the half-ass thrown together military of Command. How to track men, capture them, interrogate them, kill them. But the skills didn't come naturally to everyone, and Liam, with all of his dark thoughts and history, had been especially good at it.

When the war had come, the sitting military had split. They were already scattered around the world and even more dispersed within the borders of their own country. That's what made it all such a damn blood bath. Civilian men, wherever their location, were drafted in, went through a quickie sorry excuse for training and put out on the front lines.

No one knew why they were fighting, not really. It was like you were just defending yourself from "the opposition." There was no time to think, why am I blowing up this university? This hospital? This power plant?

Cole and Liam had been visiting Cole's family in Pennsylvania at the time it all started. So they were on the side of the Northeast by default. Having survived their first six month stint at the front, they were gathered back, sent through more intensive training and assigned to a unit of twelve. The remains of which were spread about him now.

Back then though, it took a long time before it started feeling real. Even the killing was like something out of a computer game at first. It wasn't until they were given that two day furlough between training and assignment. That was when it hit them. And the realness had been brutally hard.

Cole had been panicking. And though Liam tried to talk him down, something inside of his friend just *knew*. So they had hauled ass back to Cole's childhood home and found them all fucking lying there. Cole's dad, his two little sisters and his mom. Gassed to death. Their bodies were covered in sores. Dried blood stained the carpeting around their mouths.

A part of Cole died right then. Liam watched it happen. Hell, he could *hear* it in the quality of his friend's screaming. The way his body had sagged when Liam was forced to drag him outside. But that was what transformed Cole into such a gifted leader. After that day, a part of him was willing to die. Shit, a part of him welcomed it even. Liam knew the feeling. He recognized it immediately.

During each and every mission, Cole began taking risks that others wouldn't and that's what made him so good. Scary good. Liam only hoped that Cole still had that edge now. They would need it to complete this next mission without casualty.

Because the way he saw it, they were going in stone cold blind.

They had to strike a place they had never seen, with no tech, no helmets or night vision. On top of that, they had to face an unknown number of men of unknown training backgrounds and weapons capabilities. Plus, they were on a time table. They had to get the woman out quickly which meant they couldn't pussy foot around the whole thing like at the farmhouse disaster.

And to top it all off... Liam inhaled a breath, drew in the scent of air that blew in from beneath the edge of the tarp. They were going to have to do it all in the snow.

CHAPTER THIRTY-THREE_
HANNAH

HE DID IT. LIAM FOUND IT. AFTER OVER A WEEK'S WORTH OF
hiking and searching, making camp without the benefit of
fire, Liam had brought them to the bad place. A foot of
snow covered the ground but at least the soft white flakes
had finally stopped falling. It was sunset and the clouds
that filled the sky overhead were threatening more.

The team was assembled in a stand of trees that butted
up against a rocky hillside. They had tucked the cart in as
far as it would go under a heavy overgrowth of brush that
hung down just above them. It was good that it was so
cold. At least that was what Liam said. It forced the ones
they were hunting to use fire and that meant the location
of men and their camps was apparent from the constant
curl of smoke that rose above them.

Liam and Cole had narrowed their final destination
down to two separate plumes. One that originated much
further to the west, and one that was close, maybe two

miles further northeast. Liam and Cole then split up, each of them leaving on horseback to scout the locations. By the morning, they should all have their answer.

And Hannah could feel it down in her bones now, they were so very close. The pond with the little stream that ran into it, the one she remembered getting a drink from, it was here. She could step out from the cover and turn right and there it was, at the bottom of the next hill.

"Hey." Davey shook her shoulder a little. "You okay?"

"Yeah." Hannah gave him a smile as the light continued to fade all around them.

"Memories?"

"Something like that," Hannah conceded, but the word *memory* was a sensitive one.

She still couldn't remember anything before Andy and the running. Except for the strange doctor in his office, but that was it.

Closing her eyes now, Hannah could see Andy's face that morning. She remembered the panic. It was in the strain of his voice as he screamed at her.

Run, Hannah!

And she had run. Because she felt it, too. The terror.

The sickening flood of adrenaline hit as she looked behind them. Looked at the towering massive shining metal wall. The one that seemed to stretch for miles and miles, so smooth and high. Why were they so afraid of it? Of what was inside of it? What made her so sure she had to get away or die?

Giving her head a shake, Hannah sucked in a breath

and stretched out her right hand. She glanced briefly at the round scar, not wanting to bring any attention to it. Occasionally, it throbbed. Like it remembered being stabbed and cut. Like it was still trying to heal.

There were so many things she didn't understand. Why couldn't she remember Andy cutting her, but at the same time feel so very strongly that he had?

"Listen-" Davey broke into her reverie. "I'm sorry I brought it up. Forget it, okay?"

Pulling her in against him, he gave her a brief hug before letting go and stepping back. He thought she was remembering her time here, and the woman, but that wasn't it. That wasn't it at all.

That night was a rough one, seeming to stretch out forever in her mind. Nestled down in her sleeping bag, with Chan on one side and Ryder on the other, Hannah felt the absence of Cole and Liam acutely. Her stomach twisted, and her mind played tricks on her. Every flap of the tarp was one of them returning, but then they never came. Every sigh of the wind, every step the mule took, was agony to her.

She didn't feel like she slept at all, only drifted in and out of awareness until her neck ached and her eyes began to itch and burn. What if something happened to them out there all alone? What if Cole got hurt? What if Liam died?

When morning came and there was still no sign of

them, Hannah thought she might be sick. Her stomach heaved and the faces of the team did nothing to help her anxiety. No one spoke, not even Ryder. They all ate in silence, taking turns hiking to the top of the ridge and watching.

The low whistle that finally hummed in the air had everyone down below lifting their heads. It was Ace, he was on watch duty high above them and his signal sent a spark of nerves running through her blood stream. After a beat, they could see a rider picking his way neatly back down the rocky hillside, a black rifle clutched in one hand.

By the time Ace planted his boots back on flat ground, Cole was trotting out into the clearing in front of them.

"Cole." Hannah wanted to shout it, wanted to scream and run for him but Chan clamped a hand over her mouth, stifling her sound.

"Shhh," Chan whispered in her ear before releasing her. "We don't know enough yet."

Nodding Hannah worked to hold back the flood of feeling and instead kept her eyes glued to Cole. His progress in the open was quick. He nudged his horse into a fast trot and was soon under the protection of the trees. Throwing a leg off his gray, he handed the reins to Ace and gave a quick shake of his head.

"It wasn't the far one," he confirmed. "Just like we figured."

"What took you?" Hannah asked, not able to help herself, fingers twisting in front of her body subconsciously.

Cole's tired green eyes found hers and his face softened at the expression of worry that was written there. In two steps, he had her in his arms, gripping her close to his body a moment.

"I had to wait until dawn to watch them," he explained, pulling back to cup her face in one hand. "We had to know how many there were and what they have."

"And?" It was Davey, but they were all awaiting his answer.

"An old man and a boy." Cole glanced around, so obviously looking for Liam. He wasn't back yet. "Hand built cabin, nothing fancy. They have a hunting rifle, maybe more than one. Long story short, they won't be coming to interfere in the raid."

"You sure?" Davey again.

Cole shrugged once, then replied, "It's an awful long walk without the horse and they have no livestock. Even if they heard gunfire I doubt they'd bother coming. On the outside chance they did, it would take them half a day to get here and we'll be gone by then. Liam?"

The word hung in the air with Cole's eyes darting about the team quickly. He asked the question, but he already knew the answer. With a nod, he absorbed the obvious. No sign yet.

Hannah watched the concern furrow Cole's brow but he didn't say anything. Instead, he took his horse back from Ace and walked him over to the cart to give him a rest and a chance to eat an armful of hay. They were running low on feed, rationing it now for the animals.

Hannah walked over to him as he pulled off his saddle and hefted it to balance on the side of the cart. The gray horse ducked his head, munching greedily at the feed while the mule stamped with jealous impatience. Even beneath the jacket, Cole's shoulders were hunched with tension. It had been a long night for all of them.

"Is it so bad?" Cole whispered, once she get close. "That I want to kiss you right now? Even with him still out there?"

"No." Hannah shook her head and stepped into his embrace. "It's not so bad."

Lowering his head, Cole pressed his lips against hers, his arms wrapping tighter around her body. He was hungry for her, she could feel the way his hot mouth demanded and his hands clutched. But then there was something so guilty about it too, the way he broke off abruptly and couldn't meet her eyes.

Another low whistle sounded, and had them both jumping. Hannah couldn't help but laugh when Cole let a wide grin splash across his face. Liam was back, and they were both happy about it. Blowing out a breath, Cole released her.

Hannah nibbled on her lip for the briefest moment before planting another kiss on Cole. He staggered back as she released him and turned to make a dash for Liam. Just entering the woods, his bay horse puffing, Liam's eyes communicated their success. He didn't have to say a word, the whole team lit with excitement at his expression. They found it. They found it.

Hannah ran towards him then before he could even dismount. Leaning down low over the side of his horse he wrapped a long arm around her waist and pulled her up onto his lap. She buried her face in his neck and gripped the front of his jacket in both hands.

He wasn't dead. He hadn't been hurt out there trying to find the bad place. Her body flooded with relief. The idea of something happening to him, to either of them, had made her absolutely ill. She didn't understand it. Didn't understand how she could feel this way about both of these men at the same time.

"No public affection, remember?" Liam whispered into her ear before tipping up her chin.

"Right." Hannah agreed before she slid back down to the ground.

"Well?" Cole walked over, his eyes watching Liam.

"They're still alive," Liam exhaled it.

"They?" Cole clarified, and had the others murmuring.

"Two women." Liam's face was serious as he said it. "They have two women and there are six of them."

"Condition?" Cole pressed, as Liam swung his leg over the side and touched ground.

"The concrete structure looks like an old well house or something. It's in a small clearing with a metal cage off to one side and a fire ring in the center. But that's not where they live."

Liam walked his horse over to the cart, unsaddled him and left him to eat next to the gray. Then he grabbed his pack and pulled out a hunk of dried mutton before he picked a nearby rock to perch on. All the while, between bites and swigs of water from a canteen, Liam talked. It was the most verbal Hannah had ever heard him.

Occasionally, Cole or one of the others would interrupt, ask a few questions. But for the most part they listened, intent on the information being espoused. There were two homes, although Liam described them as "trailers," tucked further down the hill on the far side of the concrete structure. The six men and two women lived inside them.

Liam had tied his horse up last night and crept in as close as possible. It wasn't until daylight, though, that the people began moving around and leaving the trailers. That was when Liam was able to count them, note any apparent weapons and check the general atmosphere.

Hannah could tell there were things he wanted to say but didn't because she was sitting there. It was in the way he would stop mid-sentence, his dark eyes flicking to her briefly, then away. He had more information about the women and what was happening to them, but he felt uncomfortable sharing it with her.

Lifting her chin just a touch, Hannah felt he didn't give her enough credit where that was concerned. She had heard the crying before and seen the woman locked in the cage. She knew what was happening to her... or them. It was a them now, more than one.

After absorbing all of the information from Liam, Cole was quick to settle on a plan. They would attack at dusk. The fading light would give them some cover, but they'd still be able to see well enough for the initial assault. Liam and Ace would hit the larger of the two trailers around back, while Cole and Chan took the smaller. Davey would clear the fire ring, cage and concrete building.

No one argued with it. Well, almost no one. Ryder was pretty upset by the final arrangement. He'd been the one chosen to stay back and protect Hannah. It was a babysitting job, and they all knew it. At first he tried to reason with Cole, suggesting that Hannah could use a gun and stay at the cart by herself. There was no one else around for miles and the assault on the camp would keep the men there plenty occupied.

But then Cole had taken Ryder aside with Liam standing like a pillar of stone just behind him. Hannah didn't hear what they said, but at one point Liam reached around Cole to poke a hard finger into Ryder's chest, then pointed at Hannah. The words "fuck up" and "one job" were sent echoing around the woods. When Ryder was finally released from their little discussion, he wouldn't look Hannah in the eye.

The remaining hours were spent eating, drinking, checking weapons and resting. Liam actually fell asleep under the cart. The steady rise and fall of his chest under the bedroll was amazing to Hannah. How could anyone sleep in these conditions?

Even she felt a mix of excitement and dread. There were women, real actual other women so close to her now. She only hoped they were okay, only hoped all the guys made it back in one piece.

By the time dusk approached, the team was awake, geared up and ready to go. They left Hannah, Ryder and the animals behind, opting to hike the two miles to the other camp on foot. As she watched them disappear between the thick trunks of pine trees, Hannah realized she couldn't hardly hear them.

After they had gone, the only thing remaining were their boot tracks marring the fluffy white snow.

"This is bullshit," Ryder huffed.

"I'm sorry."

"It's not..." Ryder paced before turning to her. "It's not you. It's just that I should be with them."

"I know-"

"They forget I've fought every damn mission, too." He grabbed the ball cap off his head and ran a hand through his short blonde hair. "They think just because I'm younger than they are that I'm not good enough."

"I don't think-"

"But I am good enough, and they need me, Hannah." Ryder let his blue eyes lock with hers. "They need me."

"Of course they need you," Hannah agreed, quick to try to pacify him. But it turned out to be the absolute worst thing for her to say.

"Then you understand why I've got to go."

"Wait... what?"

Hannah watched his face flush with a bright happiness as he replaced his hat on his head. Ryder slipped under the cart and rustled around for a few minutes. Hannah stopped to watch him, her heart pounding in her throat. When he emerged, he was all geared up, with his black rifle in his hands and knife fixed to his belt.

"Just stay here under the cart." Ryder was panting now as he patted the pockets of his jacket and looped the strap of his gun over his shoulder. "And we will all be back, okay?"

"Ryder..." Hannah reached a hand for him, but he only winked at her before turning his back and jogging off through the trees.

And then she was alone.

"He left me," Hannah said the words aloud to no one in particular.

The horses shifted and the mule stamped, but other than that, there was no sound. Looking off through the trees, she noted how the light was waning. The sun was going down fast and more dark clouds were rolling in. The temperature was dropping and time was running out. Hannah knew she had to make a decision, had to make one right now.

Pacing to the cart, she checked her hair, stuffing it further up into her cap. They didn't want her to be anywhere near the bad place, that was obvious in every aspect of Cole's plan. They didn't want to endanger her and they also didn't want the distraction of worrying about her while they tried to do their job. But they hadn't wanted her left alone here, either.

Despite spending months by herself in these very woods, Hannah began to shake. How had she done it? All that time alone, no pants, no shelter, no food stores. Eating grass, flowers and roots. Managing to stumble across the half-chewed carcass of a rabbit and feeling absolute glorious elation at the prospect of licking the bones clean.

She didn't want to be left alone, not anymore. Not ever.

"Wait," she breathed the word, barely audible into the air. "I'm coming, too."

Suddenly, her boots had a mind of their own. They moved quickly beneath her, following the path in the snow so recently stomped out by the men ahead of her.

At first, her heart pounded in her throat, she couldn't hear anything. She could only see what was directly in front of her. Snow, boot tracks, trees, straggly bushes. But then her mind began to clear and her breathing became regular with the demands of her hike.

Around every corner, bend and break, there was nothing and no one. If she was gaining on them, she didn't know it. But they had come this way, that part wasn't hard to tell.

After what seemed a long time she heard the first pop of gunfire. It was close, closer than she would have imagined and it had her running. Her boots sank in the snow on the hillside. She stumbled a bit, lurching forward as that first shot became many.

The shooting echoed all around her, magnifying against the mountains. Sucking in air, Hannah could hear the sound of men shouting, the rapid release of more gunfire and the whistles that the team used to communicate. When she crested the hill she stopped short, dropping to her stomach to survey what played out not a hundred feet below her.

There were two women in the cage. One was standing, her hands looped around the bars, her face pressed between the metal rungs. The other one was lying in a crumpled heap at the bottom, not moving.

Davey was standing in front of them. The door to the far concrete building hung open, it was empty. He was talking to the women. Though his mouth was moving, Hannah couldn't hear what he said. The pop of gunfire continued further out, where the trailers must be, and there was more shouting.

Then Davey was kneeling down, reaching his hand into the cage, shaking the lifeless form of the woman who lay at the bottom. With his back to the concrete building, he didn't see the other man approaching, the one who was running.

Hannah's chest grew tight and she couldn't breathe. Davey didn't see him, and the woman didn't see him. They were all so caught up in each other. But then the other man was past the building, closing the distance. His arm was raised. He was pointing a gun at Davey's back.

Hannah sprang to her feet. *Davey, run, Davey!* She tried to scream the words, but nothing came out of her throat. *No. No. No.*

Two shots fired. Pop, pop.

Davey spun to look behind him, the shock clear on his

face. His eyes were wide, his mouth hanging open. Because the bad man had fallen to the ground at his feet, lying completely still and bleeding. But how? Hannah blinked. Slowly. Everything was happening so slowly.

Then just below her, Ryder came jogging out into the open. He had been hiding at the bottom of the hill. It was Ryder's gun that had fired. He had been the one to do the shooting.

Relief flooded Hannah's system. Davey was safe. She watched as Ryder came up to stand before his brother. He was all smiles even though Davey was screaming at him. She could hear him cursing and it made her smile, too. Then Davey turned his attention back to the cage and Ryder stepped back to give him room.

Hannah wiped at her face and swallowed. Then there was movement. The man on the ground was still alive. He wasn't dead. And in an instant, everything changed.

Time sped up. He lurched forward, a knife glinting in his fist as he dove for Ryder. And at the moment Hannah finally started screaming. He made contact with Ryder's back.

Over and over he drew the knife out and plunged it back in. He was so fast. So fast.

Hannah dropped to her knees as Davey swung back around in horror. His baby brother, who just a moment before had saved his life, was now the one bleeding in the snow.

It was like the world split then, right down the middle.

Hannah had experienced the sensation before. When

she'd watched Andy kneel down on the bank of a river and get his head blown off, the world had split wide. That sucking sensation, the one where the water pulls you down and seems to hold onto you, that's what it feels like.

You're trying to breathe but you can't take in any air. Your chest squeezes so tight. But then all at once it releases you, and you're swimming to the surface, kicking and fighting and dying to live.

Hannah was running. She didn't recall moving her feet but they carried her down the hill to the place where Ryder lay. Davey was holding him in his arms, screaming and rocking. Glancing over, Hannah saw the bad man. He was on his face in the slush and dirt with Cole and Chan kneeling on his back. Where had they come from?

Then she was skidding to a stop beside Ryder, looking down into his eyes and they drifted over to her, slowly. He was still alive. Barely. The blood covered the snow, melting and mixing with the mud where boots had run and bodies had fallen.

"Turn him over!" The woman from the cage was calling to them. "I'm a nurse! Turn him onto his stomach and apply pressure to the wounds! Do it!"

So then Hannah was doing it. She tugged Ryder from Davey's grasp and flipped him onto his belly. He groaned aloud which seemed to snap Davey out of his trance. Then they were both fumbling over Ryder, lifting his jacket and vest and shirt, pressing their hands over this wound and that wound. There were so many. Too many.

Hannah's hat fell off and her sweep of golden hair

dropped forward into her face as she leaned over the body. Tears rolled down her cheeks and when she looked up at Davey she saw a ghost in his place. He was so ashen.

Then Chan was beside her adding his hands to the mix and someone was calling for Ace because he was a medic and had brought a kit. But then Hannah heard screaming. The woman from the cage, she was screaming.

"Hannah?! Oh my God! Hannah?! Is that you?! Oh my God!"

The woman was reaching through the bars, as if she could only just touch Hannah and discover the truth. But when Hannah looked into her hazel eyes, she didn't recognize her. This dirty, beaten, shouting woman, who was she?

Sitting back hard on her butt, Hannah felt suddenly dizzy. The scar on her hand throbbed and she felt like she might throw up. All she could hear was the woman, see her drawn face with her one black eye and her red hair all torn and tattered. *Who are you? Should I know you?*

"What're you doing here?" Cole hissed.

He was suddenly so close, crouching down beside Hannah. Then he was yanking her up, pulling her into him, holding her tight. They stood there, with her back to the screaming woman and Ryder dying on the ground.

Out of the corner of her eye, she saw Liam kneeling on the bad man's back and Ace crouched beside Davey.

"What're you doing here?" Cole repeated, whispering it as he looked over her shoulder. "Do you know her?"

He pulled her back to arm's length, his bright green

eyes darting over her face. Hannah shook her head once, then blinked. Everything was spinning, rotating around so very slowly. And then Cole was shaking her, and shouting something, but she couldn't hear him. It was all so far away.

And then her eyes rolled back in her head, and the darkness filled her mind with a silent calm nothing.

THE FUCKER UNDERNEATH HIM KEPT TWITCHING BUT LIAM only pushed his knee further into the bastard's spine. With both of his arms wrenched up behind him and Liam's free hand holding a knife to his neck, the asshole that stabbed Ryder wasn't going anywhere. Other than that, it was utter chaos.

Ryder was bleeding out in the snow. Ace kept injecting him with shit and stuffing gauze in his back, but Liam wasn't sure it would be enough. The look on Davey's face was too much so Liam refocused his attention on Cole.

He was dragging Hannah up and back, away from the body and the work that needed to go on there. Then there was the woman in the cage, she kept shrieking Hannah's name. It was otherworldly. How did she know it?

Liam chanced a glance behind him just to be sure, but he knew he had left three men lying dead in the large trailer. Cole had confirmed two more kills in the small one and so that just left the one groaning beneath him. Let him groan, Liam thought, more would be coming his way.

Then Cole was shouting and Liam looked up. Hannah was crumpling, folding in on herself and Cole was the only thing keeping her from hitting the ground. Her head lolled to one side and her arms went limp. She passed out, she had to have just passed out.

Panic leapt quickly inside of him as he tried to talk himself down from thinking the worst. There hadn't been another gunshot, but maybe she had been stabbed, too.

"Is she bleeding?!" Liam shouted it, but he knew he couldn't get up. He was the only thing keeping this last guy in place. It took everything in him not to gut the fucker now and go to her.

"I don't know!" Cole called.

Sinking down, Cole lowered her to the snow and his hands flew all over. He opened her jacket and lifted her shirt, rolled her lifeless body to the side and let his hands feel her back and down her pants to her legs. Finally he sat back and sucked in a breath.

"No," Cole called, locking eyes with Liam. "Just passed out."

Liam's body flooded with relief and he ducked his head, trying to hide the emotion. What the fuck was Ryder doing here? And Hannah too, for that matter? He had told the kid that he had the most important job and he wasn't to fuck it up. But now they were both lying in the snow and one of them was dying. There was no doubt in Liam's mind about that.

Grabbing at the asshole still pinned beneath him, Liam began patting him down, checking for weapons and wounds. The guy jumped about six inches off the ground and screamed when Liam passed over his right shoulder. There was a bullet wound there, good to know.

"I'm going to kill that fucker!" Davey was screaming now, still watching Ace and Chan work frantically over Ryder's body. "He needs to die!"

And then Davey was lurching to his feet, staggering with his brother's blood all over him and tears running down his face. Liam's heart rate increased and he glanced to Cole who was running his fingers down Hannah's cheek. Her eyes were fluttering open and she reached up to grab his hand.

"Cole!" Liam called, and then nodded at Davey.

Cole jumped to his feet and got Davey's attention. "You can't leave him just yet, buddy. You have to stay with your brother. He's going to make it."

"He's not going to make it," Davey heaved. "Why is that fucker still breathing? I need to kill him, he needs to die."

"And he will." Cole nodded his head and put out his hands, placating. "But Ryder needs you to be with him. Why don't we let Liam work his magic, huh? Let this fucker suffer that way... you know you couldn't do it any worse."

For a moment, everything seemed to still. Davey was crying and looking from Cole to his brother's body on the ground then back to Liam. Finally, he nodded his head and turned away. Liam watched him return to

Ryder's side and, bending low, begin whispering in his ear.

Ryder didn't move. His face was turned away from Liam, so he didn't know if he was even conscious anymore. Liam's blood ran cold.

"Did you hear that, friend?" Liam leaned down to do some whispering of his own. "You and I are going to spend some quality time together."

The man only groaned as Liam stepped off of him. He kept the hood of the guy's jacket firmly in hand and yanked him up to standing. After a beat the guy's legs shook and he collapsed to his knees. Sneering in disgust Liam began to drag the asshole along in the snow.

"Where did you take them?" Liam asked, but the bastard only whimpered. "All of you sick rapist fucks have a spot right? Where was it?"

The guy's eyes went wide before he began struggling against Liam's forward progress. But Liam merely kept a smile on his face as he continued to drag the guy's kicking body through the snow.

When they neared the concrete building the bastard blanched at the sight of it. That's when Liam knew he had the right spot. Just before they crossed the threshold, Liam heard Cole's voice shout to him and so he paused.

Turning to glance over his shoulder he saw Cole standing. Hannah was braced against his legs, her eyes squeezed shut.

"Liam!" He called. "Make him feel it. Make him feel all of it."

It was a weird sort of calm, but it flowed smoothly through Liam's veins. As he straddled the other man, digging his knife deep into the gunshot wound of his shoulder, Liam knew that the man screamed. He knew he made terrible, un-Godly sounds, ones that would echo inside Liam's mind later, sometimes even waking him from his dreams. But right this minute, when he wrapped his hand over the man's neck and twisted the blade slowly inside of him, it didn't bother Liam at all.

Nope, not one little bit.

Because when Liam looked down into the man's eyes, so full of pain and shock and fear, all Liam saw was his own father staring back at him. He heard his father's voice, felt the sting of the belt buckle against his feet and legs and back. *I'm gonna make you tough son. This is for your own good. It'll make you a man.*

Well, Liam thought ruefully, it had certainly made him something. A cold fucking something.

"Where did you get them?" Liam asked. His voice was reserved, distant even.

The man had the nerve to start crying, whimpering. But it was like this with all women abusing assholes. On the outside they were all fear and control and rage, but on the inside, they were disgusting and pitiful and weak.

Liam had tortured his fair share of men, all kinds of men. And in the end, they all cried for their mama. But these ones, the weak ones, they died early... too early really. So Liam removed the knife from the guy's shoulder and instead drew it slowly down the side of his ugly face. A deep red line of blood began to flow and the man howled something awful.

With a sigh, Liam had to wait for him to stop before repeating the question. "Where did you get them?"

"Who?"

"The women."

Liam moved the knife back to the gunshot wound and dug around some more. Ryder would want the bullet if he survived. And Liam would get it for him, not a problem. Hell, he would even make it into a necklace for the kid.

"Andy!" The man screamed the name and had Liam pausing. "From Andy... from Andy."

"Andy?" Liam asked and the knife stilled in his hand. That was a damn familiar name, Cole had told him all about it.

"Yeah, yeah. Please just stop cutting me. Please."

"Keep talking." Liam withdrew the knife from the man's shoulder, but held it against his other cheek.

"He ju- ju- just showed up one day." The fucker was shaking, spittle flying from his disgusting mouth as he sputtered. "He was from the other side of that wall and he said he could get us women."

"Go on," Liam prompted, but inside he made a mental note to go back and ask more about the wall.

"He showed us where to pick them up, where he would leave them."

"And what did you give him?" Liam asked.

"Two backpacks, two- two- sleeping bags, a bow and a gun."

"An old revolver?" Liam kept his voice calm, but inside his heart was pounding, and that was nothing compared to the voice in his head. *Andy... like Hannah's dead husband, Andy?*

"Yeah. Yeah. Yeah."

"Alright." Liam flipped his knife over in his hand and then quick as anything, he swiped off the tip of the guy's nose. The answering scream was deafening. "Let's talk more about this wall."

A word from the author:

Cliffhanger endings... I apologize. When I first wrote this book (several years ago) I was still learning my craft, and many books later, I no longer use this technique. However, this is a really great story and I promise it's worth an abrupt ending (or two) I promise I don't do it throughout the entire series.

And besides, Book 2 is right at your fingertips.

Go get it now...

CHASING TRUTH

Join my ARC Team!

Click on the link - ARC TEAM - LK MAGILL

Want to know when the next book is ready?

Sign up for an email notification here...

LK MAGILL NEWSLETTER

Reviews, pretty please...

Each and every positive review makes a huge difference. Be it Amazon, Kobo, iBooks, Barnes and Noble, Book Bub, Goodreads; no matter the retailer, I read and appreciate them all.

Thank you and I hope to see you in the future.

Websites:

www.lkmagill.com

Like me on Facebook:
https://fb.me/LKMagill1

Follow me on Instagram:
https://www.instagram.com/lk.magill.author

Follow me on Amazon:
http://amazon.com/author/lkmagill

Standalone novels:

VANISH ME

The Captive Series:

THE CAPTIVE BORN - Book One

THE CAPTIVE MISSING - Book Two

THE CAPTIVE RISING - Book Three

Outlasting Series:

OUTLASTING AFTER - Book One

CHASING TRUTH - Book Two

SURVIVING THE WALL - Book Three

BREAKING BEFORE - Book Four

TAKING TOMORROW - Book Five

FINDING FOREVER - Book Six

Made in the USA
Las Vegas, NV
28 August 2021